The Proving Gun

Also by Ray Hogan
JACKMAN'S WOLF
CONGER'S WOMAN
MAN WITHOUT A GUN
HONEYMAKER'S SON
THE DOOMSDAY MARSHAL

The Proving Gun

RAY HOGAN

DOUBLEDAY & COMPANY, INC.
GARDEN CITY, NEW YORK
1975

All of the characters in this book are fictitious,
and any resemblance to actual persons, living or
dead, is purely coincidental.

Library of Congress Cataloging in Publication Data

Hogan, Ray, 1908–
    The proving gun

    I. Title.
PZ4.H716Pr [PS3558.03473] 813'.5'4
ISBN 0-385-11177-0
Library of Congress Catalog Card Number 75-9224

FOR MY FATHER—

Thomas Newton Hogan

The Proving Gun

Levitt glanced at the men crouched around him in the shadows behind the Caprock Cattlemen's Bank. . . . Deke Harvey, the wet-nosed kid from Texas he'd known only a few weeks; Rufe Pearce, as tough a hardcase as he'd ever come across, but a harebrain who was always too damned quick to use the forty-five he carried on his hip; Al Kirk, a long-time acquaintance but who, like him, was getting old and slow.

Levitt's mouth curved scornfully. Except for Kirk, he could have done a hell of a lot better when it came to rounding up partners for what he hoped would be his last job—one that would provide the stake he needed to cross the border into Mexico and retire, once and for good. But J. J. Levitt had found himself with little choice. The bunch he'd ridden with much of his life and accordingly knew well, were gone—either dead or in the pen, and picking the men to side him had been a matter of potluck.

He'd worked out his plan to rob the Caprock Bank very carefully, wanting no slip-ups, no mistakes, knowing deep in his mind that it would be his last job regardless of how it turned out. He'd simply grown too old for the life he was leading—one of riding the trails, staging a holdup whenever he was in need of money, and always dodging the law, and while fifty-one was no advanced age, a man pursuing the routine, year in and year out, wore down mighty fast.

Unlike others he'd known, Levitt was smart enough to admit it—if only to himself. He'd always been able to see his own weaknesses and took pride in the fact that he never fooled himself where he, personally, was concerned. Just such had brought him to Caprock and its rich little bank; it was time to quit and the wherewithal to do so lay within it and then he could retire comfortably south of the border.

"When're we making a move?"

It was Pearce, impatient, hard to handle and reckless. Rufe was about thirty-five, maybe even forty, Levitt reckoned, and had been around long enough to learn a few things, but seemingly he had not.

"Soon as it's full dark," Levitt murmured wearily.

He looked beyond the corner of the bank to the narrow street that separated the rows of structures. Many of the shopkeepers had lit their lamps, and light spilling through the windows lay in yellow splashes across the dust. . . . But there was still too much glow in the sky. Best to wait another ten or fifteen minutes.

"J.J.—"

Levitt turned his attention to Al Kirk, a small, wizened shape in the murk. He could depend on Kirk, he knew. At such moments Al was like a steel wire and cool as a winter breeze along the Bozeman Trail.

"Yeh?"

"That there safe you looked over, any chance it'll be closed? Getting kind of late and maybe them bank fellows'll be locking up."

"Won't make no difference. If we're lucky it'll still be open, if it ain't we'll just have to make them open it. Be three men in there, figuring there ain't no customers, which is another reason we're stalling. I'd as soon there'd not be somebody else around 'cepting them."

"Why're you worrying about that?" Pearce grumbled. "Be all the same to me—"

"Won't to me!" Levitt snapped. "I don't want no ruckus. We work this like I got it planned and we can be halfway to the border before anybody knows what's happened. You got that tow-sack, Deke?"

Harvey stirred. "Sure have," he drawled. "Just waiting to be filled plumb full with all them greenbacks and gold eagles and silver dollars—"

"Just be goddam sure you get it all," Pearce muttered.

"Don't fret none about that. I—"

"Somebody's coming," Kirk warned quietly, pulling his red neckerchief up over the lower half of his face.

Levitt had caught the sound too, had raised his hand for silence as he drew back farther into the darkness behind the building. The measured thud of boot heels beating on the sun-baked ground was near—too near.

The steps drew closer. Abruptly the tall shape of a man angling through the night toward the street materialized. He was little more than a stride away. Levitt saw Pearce draw up slowly. Alarm rocked through him. He reached out hurriedly and laid a restraining hand on Rufe's arm. Pearce hesitated, and then as the man moved on by unnoticing, he settled back, his pistol making a soft, leathery scrape when he returned it to its holster. Levitt waited until the passer-by had rounded the far corner of the bank and disappeared from sight.

"What the hell's the matter with you?" he demanded in a hoarse, angry whisper, turning on Pearce. "You wanting

3

to spoil this whole thing? If you'd laid into that jasper, you'd've started something for certain!"

"Only aimed to buffalo him was he to see us—"

"And most likely ended up pulling the trigger on that iron you drawed. I'm telling you again, Rufe, there ain't going to be no gunplay! There's a marshal and a couple of deputies and a big passel of real public-spirited citizens all ready to jump astraddle of us if we give them a reason. One shot'll bring them like buzzards spotting a carcass—I know because I took a whole week looking things over."

"All right, all right," Rufe said in his dry, dissatisfied way. "When're we going to do something? I'm plenty tired of squatting here in the dark."

Levitt glanced at the sky, dark now with a few stars beginning to show. He shifted his attention then to the street. It lay in silence, the only sound being the faraway barking of a dog.

"Reckon it's time," he said. "You all just take it real slow and careful-like and things'll work out just like I figured."

Rising, Levitt crossed to the rear of the bank, the other men falling in behind him. Reaching the door he halted, waiting while Pearce, Deke Harvey and Kirk took their assigned places to his left where they would not be seen, and then rapped firmly on the metal-braced panel.

A muffled voice from the interior of the building responded immediately. "Who's there?"

"Stagecoach driver," Levitt replied. "Got a strongbox I was told to leave with you for safekeeping."

A key rattled in the door's lock and a moment later the heavy panel swung inward, framing an elderly man wearing round, steel-rimmed glasses in a rectangle of light.

"Strongbox? I don't recollect anybody saying—"

"Just step back and keep quiet," Levitt cut in briskly,

drawing his pistol and jamming the muzzle into the man's belly. "Don't aim to hurt nobody—and we won't long as you do what you're told."

The banker retreated under the prodding of Levitt's gun, his features reflecting shock and disbelief and then fear as Kirk and the others crowded into the room.

"This here's a holdup," Rufe Pearce said, grinning broadly. "We're going to just help ourselves to everything in that there safe of your'n."

Levitt nodded to Deke Harvey, gesturing toward the thick, metal door of the box, standing open. "Get busy, kid."

The young outlaw, face shining with sweat, eyes bright from excitement, trotted across the room to the safe. Levitt turned his attention to Kirk.

"Best you get up front, Al," he said.

Everything was going as he'd planned; no fuss, no re- sistance—just a quiet, little business transaction. There were no customers and the only possible complications would arise if someone entered the building from the street.

"Lock the door," he added to Kirk, and drew up sud- denly. There should be two more men in the bank— employees. Where the hell were they?

As if in reply to his unvoiced question, the missing clerks rose to their feet from behind a counter where they had taken refuge. Both were young men and each, apparently having second thoughts as to the wisdom of remaining hid- den, had his arms lifted.

Rufe Pearce was conscious only of their abrupt, unex- pected appearance. Standing beside Levitt, he spun. The weapon in his hand blasted twice. Both men staggered, fear blanking their faces as they crumpled and went down.

Startled yells sounded in the street at the crash of Pearce's gun, and immediately there was a pounding of feet as all who were in hearing distance paused in whatever they were doing to rush toward the bank.

Levitt cursed wildly. Shoving the banker aside roughly, he wheeled, starting for the rear door of the building. Deke Harvey was there ahead of him, darting through the opening into the darkness beyond and moving for the waiting horses. Gunshots ripped through the still rolling echoes of Rufe's shots as someone in the street fired blindly through the window at Al Kirk, setting up more echoes and a clattering of shattered glass.

Levitt plunged through the doorway with Pearce on his heels, Kirk a step behind the latter. They broke out into the alleyway as another spatter of shots, coming from inside the bank, hammered in their ears.

"Split up!" Levitt shouted as they raced to reach the horses. "Them buttes south of here—we'll meet there!"

"These here horses ain't going to make it another mile unless'n they get some rest," Al Kirk said as they halted on the crest of a low hill near midmorning of the following day. Pointing to a settlement lying silent in the strong sunlight a mile or so to their left, he added: "Best we lay over for a spell there in that town—whatever its name is."

"Mimbres Crossing," Levitt supplied woodenly.

Everything had gone wrong at Caprock. Not only did they now have two murders hanging over their heads and a posse on their trail, but young Deke Harvey, in the sudden and unexpected turn of events, had in his wild haste to get out of the bank, dropped the sack into which he was dumping the money. The whole, carefully planned affair had been for nothing.

6

"You know the place? Ain't a bad-looking town."

Levitt nodded dispiritedly. "I was here once—for a few days."

"It got a bank?" Pearce asked, shifting on his saddle. "It's kind of prosperous-looking."

Again Levitt nodded. "Lot of ranchers do business there. Same with some homesteaders."

"The bank fat as you claim the one in Caprock was?"

"Like as not—"

Pearce swore loudly. "Then why in the hell didn't we pick it instead the other'n? We must be a hundred miles closer to the border."

Levitt turned, studied Pearce with cold, level eyes. "Because the sheriff here once done me a favor. Always told myself I'd leave his town alone."

"Well, he ain't never done me no favor," Rufe declared. "Now, I figure we got one, maybe two days' jump on that posse, figuring that blind trail we give them to follow. That'll give us plenty of time to bust this dump wide open. You say yes to that, Al?"

Kirk shrugged, wiped at the sweat on his face. "Well, we sure got to do something. I'm flat broke, and with that posse—"

"How about you, kid?" Pearce continued, turning to Deke Harvey.

"Whatever you all aim to do is jake with me—"

Rufe placed his attention on Levitt. "We're all three for it. What do you say?"

Levitt's shoulders stirred. "Don't see as we've got much choice. Could be that sheriff—name was Luke Jones—is gone by now, anyway."

"Good. Let's get down there. We can ride straight in and—"

"Nope," Levitt cut in bluntly, taking charge again, "that'll mean more killings and you've done enough of that, Rufe. I don't want another posse tailing us. . . . We'll do it my way, and at night."

"How long was you around here for, J.J.?" Kirk asked.

"About a week. Got myself sort of acquainted, then backed off of what I was figuring to do. Bank's on the west side of the street. Ain't setting on a corner like the one in Caprock, but I recollect there's a vacant lot alongside it. Livery stable's close by."

"We could hole up there, let the horses get back in shape—"

"Wouldn't be smart. Luke Jones used to make the rounds regular like. Kept a real clean town. . . . There's a grove of trees to the south with a creek running through it —Mimbres Creek it's called. Plenty of grass for the horses and lots of brush where we could hide out."

"Nag of mine ain't got much left in him," Deke said, glancing critically at his horse. "Think laying over the rest of the day and the night'll fix him up so's he can make it to Mexico?"

"Could maybe wait out another night," Kirk said. "Ain't likely that Caprock posse'll be catching up, not for a couple of days, like Rufe's saying."

"Expect that's right," Levitt agreed. "Best we just take things as they come, howsomever. Right now let's find ourselves a place in that picnic grove and climb off these saddles. Then we can do some deciding."

2

Tom Sutton smiled, nodding understandingly to Luke Jones. The old lawman was long on giving advice, some of which had a familiar ring—like echoes out of his schooldays past—but Tom always listened patiently and respectfully. Luke was a fine old man and, insofar as he was concerned could be forgiven most anything.

Leaning against the front wall of the jail, soaking in a measure of the warm, midmorning sunshine, Sutton glanced along Mimbres Crossing's main street. It was a good town; prosperous, orderly and with no serious problems. And it would be his town by the end of the year if everything went as expected for Luke Jones was turning in his star and retiring, and as deputy, Tom would automatically step into the older man's boots and serve until the regular election which would come that following November.

"But you won't have no trouble then," Luke had said when Sutton expressed doubt. "Three quarters of the votes in this county come right out of this town—and that'll be more'n enough to elect you."

Tom was only fairly sure. As Jones's deputy for only a year and no lawman experience other than that; just turned twenty-one, and the son of a man who had died of drunkenness on the steps of the Poor Man's Saloon—the town's lowest rated establishment—he had certain, understandable qualms. Now, shifting his gaze to the elderly sheriff slouched in the doorway nearby and also enjoying the sun's warmth, he shook his head.

"There's a few folks around here who don't figure I can cut the mustard, far as being sheriff's concerned. Could be enough of them to beat me out."

Jones—lean, gray, with a narrow, sharp face and small, snapping black eyes—spat into the dust. He threw a disdainful glance toward the general store. "You're talking about Karl Jergenson, I expect, and Jess Fallon and a half a dozen others. Hell with them—and you best start getting used to have some folks against you. It's natural. A man can't please everybody no matter how hard he tries. Want you to remember that. You're going to tromp on somebody's corns whatever you do."

"There any chance they can all get together and keep me from taking over when you quit the first of the year?"

"Nope. Deputy always steps right up and pins on the star if something happens to the sheriff. Way it's always been. Anyhow, I've done hashed it out with John Kilborn. He's right with us, and being the mayor, that counts for plenty.

"Stop your worrying, boy! Don't get a man nowheres and just stirs up his bowels. The job's your'n. You already put in a year or better learning the ropes, and I'll be around for a few more months, then after that you'll have till election to show them you can do it."

"Reckon that's what's bothering me—proving myself. We haven't come up against any bad problems—not since I've been your deputy, and if I had to use my gun—"

"A man proves himself a good lawman in a lot of ways, not by just showing how good he can use a pistol. Being able to get the job done without drawing his iron counts for more to my way of looking at it. That's probably what's chawing on Jergenson and them others, I reckon. They ain't sure how you'll do was you to someday come up against a hardcase with a fast gun."

Jones hesitated and turned his attention to the Poor Man's Saloon at the opposite end of the street, a frown on his leathery features. Tom shifted his eyes to that point. The Avery brothers, Pete and Gabe, and a newly arrived friend of theirs called Buffalo Finch, from up Kansas way it was said, were passing the time loafing, as usual, alongside the small building.

Luke Jones's glance was not on them, however, but had settled instead on a small, wiry man wearing faded range clothing, run-down boots and a red neckerchief, who had come out of the saloon and was standing on the narrow landing that fronted the building. He had evidently just purchased a bottle of whiskey and was carrying it by the neck.

"Somebody you know?"

Luke shrugged, continuing to watch the slightly built man as he crossed the street and disappeared into the passageway between Huffman's Feed & Seed Store and the Winchester Hotel.

"Somebody I don't know," he murmured, coming back around. "Always sets me to wondering, but I reckon he's just some cowhand riding through. Thing like that gets to be a habit—puzzling over who a stranger is and what he's wanting—and that ain't good when you come right down to it. Man oughtn't to be suspecting everybody he don't know."

"I'm not so sure about that. Nobody'll catch him napping if he's that way."

"Possible," the lawman agreed, and nodded to a woman

passing by on the board sidewalk. "Fellow wearing a star can't be too careful, and he sure wants to remember to never be scared of anything except of not being scared. Minute he stops being that way is when he's starting to get careless. I don't mean the running kind of scared, I mean the kind that keeps him sort of strung out tight and ready for anything.

"And he hadn't ought to be the kind that's always borrowing trouble, either. Most of the time it ain't there, and whatever it is he's stewing about'll just blow on over. When was the last time we had a big problem—the shooting kind, I mean?"

Tom shook his head. "Only trouble we've had around here since I've been your deputy is some thieving and the scrapes the Averys've got into."

"Exactly. Been two years before that—more'n three altogether in fact, if you're looking to be close. There was a fracas between some cowhands from Ben Starr's Spear Ranch and a bunch of Jonathan Wilson's hayshakers—one of them there rancher-sodbuster things. They had it out in that corral behind McCandless' livery stable and a galoot working for Starr who fancied himself some kind of a gunslinger up and got himself killed."

"Been over three years, all right," Sutton murmured. "That was before Pa and me moved here, after Ma died."

"Well, anyway, that ended it. Ain't been no big trouble around here between the ranchers and the homesteaders since. Nowadays the Starrs and the Wilsons are the best of friends. Same goes for all the others. They get together for sociables and there's even been a couple of marryings between them."

"Expect you've had plenty to do with the peace that's between them."

"Yeh, maybe so, but it'd be the same no matter who was wearing the star—and wearing it right. Lawman doing his job the way he's supposed to, why, things in a town just naturally goes smooth."

Traffic along the street had increased. Being the week-end, many of the outlying residents were coming in to do their trading, and saddle horses, buggies and wagons pulled up to the hitchracks along the dusty way had increased in number.

The tinkle of piano music was coming from the Western Star, the settlement's largest saloon, despite the early hour, and the clang of the anvil in Harley Hopkin's blacksmith shop was like the measured tolling of a bell on the warm air. Off to the south of town, in the direction where most of the homesteads lay, a jackass brayed noisily, while overhead crows straggled across the clean blue of the sky in raucous disorder.

"Like I said, best you quit worrying about things," Jones continued. "Folks are only wanting a man who can do the job for them, and far as I'm concerned, you're him."

The lawman paused again as a pair of matched blacks drawing a shiny black surrey filled with several young girls and a slightly older woman cut into the street from the vacant lot alongside the jail. Both men came to attention, nodding politely, Sutton's attention centering mainly on the woman who smiled indifferently to his greeting as the vehicle rolled on.

"Miss Bain and her young ladies heading for the picnic grove," Luke Jones murmured fretfully. "Don't know what kind of learning she can give them down there every Saturday that she can't give them weekdays at the schoolhouse, but I reckon she knows what she's doing."

"Reads to them from books—poetry and stories about

knights and kings, and things like that—stuff she don't get a chance to teach in regular school. They're sort of a special class."

"That's sure the truth," the sheriff said, rubbing at his jaw, "all of them being the daughters of the big muckity-mucks around here! You don't see none of the ordinary folks's kids there. They ain't got the time for such high-toned learning. Have to stay home and help with the housework on weekends."

Tom grinned. "Sounds like you don't approve of Olive Bain's special class for young ladies."

"I don't care one way or another about that part of it—it's her taking them down to that grove that bothers me. Lots of drifters and saddle tramps ride through there, heading for the border. Something could happen to them girls and we'd never know nothing about it till it was all over and too late."

"Olive's real careful—"

"Maybe she is but what could one woman do about anything—especially her? Hell, I bet she ain't much older than them girls herself, and they ain't but sixteen, maybe seventeen. I'd feel a lot better about it if she'd hold them fancy classes back in the schoolhouse where teaching's supposed to be done."

The surrey had crossed the street, passing between two of the several houses that lined the far side, and was now hidden by the last structure as it made its way toward the grove.

"Think I'll have me a little talk with Miss Olive Bain," Jones said thoughtfully, eyes on the point where the teacher and her pupils had disappeared. "Sure would hate for something to happen to them girls—and her, of course.

Which puts me in mind of something—how're you and the teacher coming along?"

Tom Sutton shrugged. "We're not. Olive made it plenty plain she don't figure being a lawman is much of a job. Somebody like a lawyer or a doctor—professional man she calls them—is what she thinks girls ought to marry. Includes herself in that, I expect."

Luke Jones snorted. "Professional man, eh! Maybe she ought to stop and think about them girls she's put notions like that into. Ain't none of their pas anything but ranchers or sodbusters that've grubbed their way up to being somebody—"

"Except for Henry Maxwell at the bank and Jergenson. Their daughters are in the class."

"That's two out of five, and Jergenson wasn't nothing but a wagon peddler before he got enough cash together to open that store of his'n."

"Well, it's how she thinks—and I'm not losing any sleep over it."

"Maybe you ought. She's a mighty fine-looking young woman and she'd make you a good wife—just needs a little straightening out, that's all."

Sutton smiled visualizing anyone, particularly himself, straightening out strong-minded Olive Bain. He drew up, pulling away from the wall of the jail and glanced toward the livery stable.

"Think I'll take a walk down to McCandless' place, have a look at my horse. Seems to be favoring a leg. Noticed it yesterday."

"Frog needs cleaning out, likely. You ain't rode him enough lately for anything else," Jones said. "Reckon I'll trot along with you, get my sorrel. I'm going to ride down and have that talk with the teacher while it's fresh on my mind—unless, maybe, you'd like to do it."

"No thanks," Sutton said promptly. "You're still the sheriff—and that makes it your job. . . . Let's go."

3

Waiting patiently for the girls to settle themselves on the lap robe from the Henshaw surrey, Olive Bain looked out over the land beyond the grove. Grassy and green, with a distant background of white-streaked, rose-colored buttes, it rolled away in gentle swells only periodically marred by a solitary cedar, clumps of rabbit brush or patches of needle-sharp yucca.

Mimbres Crossing was the last place in the world that Olive had expected to one day find herself—and a far cry from the street market in Cincinnati where her parents owned and operated a fruit and vegetable stand and where she, the eldest of seven children, had grown up. Times were always hard and the brunt of caring for three brothers and an equal number of sisters while her father and mother struggled to eke out a living for all, had fallen upon her slim shoulders.

She had been cook, nurse, doctor, disciplinarian and confessor to them all and, understandably, had grown heartily sick of such an existence—so much so that it had impelled her despite the toll of endless drudgery, to get a sufficient education by attending night classes to become a schoolteacher. At the age of nineteen she had, without regret, removed herself from the squalid quarters, rejoicing in the fact that among other things, she would never again hear herself called *Ollie,* a diminutive she had come to hate.

A background of such shallowness could only leave its strong mark on her and thus she had come away with a deep desire to help other girls, to see that they became something more than mere household slaves and were instead aware of the finer things in life—the *savoir-faire* as she termed it—that the right atmosphere and the proper exposure to culture would provide.

No girl should be compelled to assume the responsibilities that had faced her from the time when she was of little more than walking age. There was more to life than that, and inducing young girls growing into womanhood to realize the fact became her destiny.

The parting with her family had not been a tearful one. With the few clothes she had managed to provide by her own skill with a needle and thread, a certificate declaring her an accredited educator safely in hand, Olive had simply bade all farewell and set out for her destination, a small town in far distant New Mexico Territory—barely civilized so she had been warned—where she would answer the call for a competent schoolteacher.

It had not been as bad as expected. The settlement was not so small after all, was exceptionally clean and devoid of the riff-raff and thieves that hung around the market in Cincinnati. The residents were friendly and the school itself, a large fort-like house that had been the home of one of the town's early settlers, had been remodeled to fit the needs of the children.

Her classes weren't large—a dozen or so in the primary grades, about the same number of high school level, five of which, to her delight, responded readily to the invitation she extended offering a class in refinement and culture for young ladies that would be conducted on Saturdays.

It was disappointing, however, that the five enrollees were all daughters of the well-to-do, and the girls she hoped most to reach, ones from the middle and lower classes—terms Olive detested using—could only be enlightened during established school hours and even then, when some emergency arose in their homes and they were forced to be absent, not at all.

But Olive Bain did the best she could to raise the level of her pupils' horizons, one and all, and while there was great satisfaction in knowing she was meeting with a degree of success, her "special young ladies" as she liked to term the five girls gathered before her now—Dulcie Henshaw, Amy Starr, Katie Jergenson, Charity Maxwell and Lucy Teague—were her shining examples of erudition and grace.

Already they were looking far ahead, believing firmly in her admonition that it was just as easy for a girl to fall in love and marry a wealthy, influential man, who could give her the finer things in life, as it was to bind herself to a poor one where she would become only ordinary—a housewife and a mother, perhaps many times over, and slated for a hopeless future.

It was not an impossible dream, she insisted often. Why not find that kind of life with some important man who would take her to one of the great cities like New York, or Boston or perhaps New Orleans—or even Washington, where all the important persons who ran the country were to be found? Professional, wealthy men could make their homes anywhere they wished; why not in a place where there was opera and stage plays and fine libraries to be enjoyed?

Olive was wholly in agreement with Mr. Daniel Webster and many times to drive home her point, had quoted his words on the subject of the West: *What do we want with this worthless area? It is a region of savages and wild beasts, dust, cactus and prairie dogs. I will never vote one cent of public treasury to place it one inch nearer . . .*

On the first occasion of her voicing Mr. Webster's utterance, one of the girls, Amy Starr, had repeated it along with certain other ideas advanced by her teacher, to her family. Mr. Starr, a strong, forceful man and successful rancher, had gone into a state of rage and angrily denounced her for putting such thoughts into his daughter's mind.

But it had gone no further than just the denunciation as Mrs. Starr, perhaps a bit wistful herself for the new, broad vistas being opened up for Amy, had interceded in her behalf and the matter was forgotten.

"Miss Bain—"

At Charity Maxwell's high-pitched voice—Olive was struggling to teach the banker's daughter to modify her tones, drop them a few octaves—she nodded, smiling. Her pupils were settled and awaiting her. Opening one of the books she had brought along, Olive touched each of the girls with her eyes.

"I thought we should start today with a verse from John Donne who, you will recall, lived in the earlier part of the seventeenth century."

"He was English," Lucy Teague volunteered.

"Yes, and he loved his country very much. He also wrote beautiful poetry and this is from a poem of his that I like very much. It is titled simply, 'Song.' I shall read the first stanza.

"'Go and catch a falling star,
Get with child a mandrake root,
Tell me where all past years are,
Or who cleft the Devil's foot;
Teach me to hear mermaid's singing,
Or to keep off envy's stinging,
And find
What wind
Serves to advance an honest mind.'

"Now, I would like for you to think about that for a few minutes, recalling the words to your mind and deciding what the author meant. Afterwards we'll discuss it. When we've finished we'll read more from Henry Van Dyke's 'The Blue Flower,' taking up where we left off last week."

J. J. Levitt took a pull from the bottle of whiskey Al Kirk had brought back from town and thoughtfully studied the group of girls clustered about their young teacher. Close beside him in the screening brush he heard Rufe Pearce swallow noisily.

"Lah-de-dah!" the gunman murmured. "Ain't that as fancy a passel of females as ever you laid eyes on?"

Levitt barely heard, just as he was paying little attention to the words being spoken by the teacher as she read from a book. His mind was following more practical lines. Here, undoubtedly, were the prized daughters of the town's most important families—the rich ones—otherwise they'd be home helping their mas with housework and such.

"'. . . Have pity on me,' she cried, 'and save my life for the sake of the God of Purity! I am also a daughter of the true religion which is taught by the Magi—'"

The voice of the teacher droned on. J.J. helped himself

to another swig of the liquor and Pearce swallowed again and laughed in a low, anxious way. Deke Harvey stirred.

"What the hell's she reading about, anyway?"

"Who cares?" Pearce replied hoarsely. "Give me some of that rotgut, Levitt."

J.J. passed the bottle to Rufe. . . . Five girls. . . . Ten thousand dollars each—fifty thousand dollars! The thought staggered him. *Fifty thousand dollars!* And it would be easy—a lot simpler than robbing a bank or holding up a stagecoach. Grab a man's kid, especially his daughter—the young and tender kind like these—and he'd come across mighty goddam quick. . . . And with his share of that much money he could live like a king in Mexico.

"Let's go a-visiting," Pearce said, rising slightly.

"No," Levitt said quietly, laying a restraining hand on the man's shoulder. "Just stay put. I got me an idea."

"Hell with your ideas. Ain't none of them worked yet. I aim to get—"

"Shut up, Rufe," Kirk cut in coldly, and then as Pearce settled back into the brush, added, "Go ahead, J.J., what're you thinking?"

"Just this. We got us a easy chance to clean up big right here. Ought to make us ten thousand dollars apiece."

"Ten thousand dollars!" Deke echoed in an awed voice.

"That's right. All any of us'll need to keep us living high on the hog for the rest of our lives—and we can get it without holding up no bank."

"Yeh? How?" Pearce asked skeptically.

"Real easy. We just grab them girls, make their papas pay us to turn them loose."

Several long minutes of silence followed Levitt's words,

and then Harvey said: "Kidnap them gals—that what you're meaning?"

"You think of a better way to get a lot of cash quick?"

"Sure a lot of cash, all right," Kirk said slowly. "Maybe more'n they can raise. . . . You figure we got time enough for something like that? Best we be looking for that Caprock posse to show up sometime tomorrow—just to be on the safe side—and I ain't anxious to be around here when—"

"We'll be gone from here by tonight, way I've got it worked out," Levitt answered, attention again on the young teacher who was continuing to read from her book.

Rufe Pearce sighed deeply. "That little yellow-haired—she sure is pretty. I'd as soon—"

"Going to have to find a place where we can hole up with them," Kirk said, ignoring the gunman. "You got that figured out too?"

"Yep. From what you said about the looks of things after going and getting that liquor, ain't nothing changed. We'll use the schoolhouse. It's on the other side of town. It was some jasper's house in the old days and they went and made a school out of it. There'll be nobody around there this time of the week. We can take them there and wait for their pas to fetch us the cash."

"That's only half of it," Pearce said. "How do we get away? You think them counter-jumpers are just going to let us ride out with all that money once they got their kids back? Like hell they will!"

"They won't try nothing—not if we've got us a hostage."

Al Kirk wagged his head. "Maybe not but dragging one of them along'll slow us down to beat hell—and I got the feeling we'll be wanting to get to the border mighty fast."

"Only need her for a couple hours—long enough to let us

23

get a good start—then we can let her go. That there teacher'll make the best hostage. Being older she more'n likely won't do a lot of squalling."

"About all she'd be good for," Pearce muttered. "It's a cinch she won't be worth nothing in money. Probably ain't got a pot or a window to throw it out of, either. Now, was we to take along that yellow-haired gal you can bet her pa'd walk plenty soft when it come to."

"Best we do like J.J. says," Kirk broke in. "How we going about doing it?"

Levitt settled back, satisfied. He had feared opposition to his idea—one that would surely guarantee him all the money he would ever need for his remaining years—but the others had all come through. Now all he had to do was make the plan work, for one thing was certain in his mind: this would be his last chance to gain independence and a life of ease in Mexico.

"Won't be nothing hard," he said. "We'll circle around, spread out. We can close in on them easy that way without them spotting us and trying to run."

"They'll do a lot of hollering—"

"Let them. This here grove's too far from town for anybody to hear. We'll load them in that surrey. Deke, you'll do the driving. Me and Al and Rufe'll be riding alongside."

"You said that there schoolhouse was on the other side of town. Ain't somebody liable to see us when we cross?"

"Not if we keep in the trees and do the crossing on below here. I'll lead the way. Rest of you just follow me."

"We tying and gagging them?" Rufe asked.

"If we have to but I don't think it'll be needful. They're all going to be mighty scared and they'll do just what they're told. Expect that teacher'll see to that." Levitt paused, turned and faced Pearce squarely. His features

24

were grim. "I want you to get this in your head, Rufe—you're to keep your hands off them girls, and you're to forget about that gun you're wearing."

Pearce bristled. "By God, I don't have to take any orders from—"

"You're taking them from me right here and now, else you can ride on. It was you that messed up our chances back there in Caprock by shooting down them two jaspers when it wasn't necessary. I ain't standing for you pulling no bonehead stunt like that again. If somebody happens to come along and gets curious and maybe starts asking questions, you leave it to me. Hear?"

"Talking ain't going to do no good if we run across some jaybird and—"

"I'll do the deciding about it. Main thing is I want you to stay out of it—clean out it."

"It's my neck, too—"

"I'm not saying it ain't. It's only that I can't trust you using your head none. I figure this is going to be the only chance I'll get to set things up for myself, and I'll tell you right here and now, Rufe, if you pull some fool thing and queer it for me—I'll kill you."

Pearce stiffened and his dark eyes hardened. And then he shrugged.

"It's your party, friend."

Levitt nodded crisply and glanced to the other men. "You both all set? You know what you're to do?"

Harvey and Al Kirk made their acknowledgment.

"Then let's get at it," Levitt said. "And while you are, keep remembering you're going to be rich when it's all done and over—so don't make no slip-ups."

4

McCandless' livery stable stood at the end of the town's main street, and Sheriff Luke Jones, astride his venerable sorrel, paused as he rode out into the bright sunshine. One hand resting on the horn, the other on the cantle of his saddle, he half turned, letting his glance run the rows of buildings lining each side.

The Cattlemen's Bank . . . Jergenson's General Store . . . Western Star Saloon . . . Adams's Gun & Saddle Shop . . . The Winchester Hotel . . . Rosebud Cafe . . . Miss Nickerson's Ladies & Childrens Shop . . . Huffman's Feed & Seed Store—the dozen or so other establishments that made up the settlement. They were like old friends, familiar and comforting, looking back at him from their glass-window eyes and worn façades.

Mimbres Crossing had been good to him, and in turn he'd given it his best over the years that he had served, and he reckoned neither he nor the town had cause to complain. He'd ridden in one day a man adrift and at loose ends after forsaking a sterile homestead in a part of the country where the land ran flat and formless from sunrise to sunset, and pleased by the sight of towering mountains, rugged canyons and startlingly green valleys, had decided here was where he would finish his stay on earth.

It was a fortunate decision for both Luke Jones and Mimbres Crossing. He was searching for a new start, a place to put down roots and the town was in need of a lawman. He had taken over, and being a methodical man with a single purpose in mind, soon cleaned up the problems of lawlessness that plagued the inhabitants and remained to become a permanent member of the settlement and the continual wearer of the town's, and later, the county's law badge.

Now it was all coming to a close. Like one of the great pines on the slopes of the nearby hills felled at last by time and the elements, so also had the years overtaken him. The day was at hand to step aside, yield to the inevitable, make room for a younger man—one in whom he could place full trust and confidence.

But he was not abandoning his town entirely; he was merely passing on his authority and star, and hanging up his gun for a quiet life of ease and satisfaction on a small piece of ground just below the settlement—thus he would always be around.

The old Evans place, folks called it, and while he would have no need for the full hundred and sixty acres it entailed, he would make good use of the small house the homesteader had built and then abandoned, and the bit of the whole that had been devoted to a vegetable garden.

He planned to recultivate that area, plant corn, melons, vegetables and a few fruit trees and leave the remainder as it was, lush with grama and buffalo grass, for the sorrel to pasture on. There was ample water from Mulehead Creek, an offshoot of the Mimbres that angled across the property, so he'd have no problem there—and what if someday it did dry up? He wouldn't mind toting a few buckets from the main stream; it would be something else to do, something to help pass the time.

But Luke reckoned he'd find himself busy enough. Like

27

as not Tom Sutton would be coming to see him pretty often for advice, and maybe even for a little help although it had been a long spell since there'd been any serious trouble in town. Of late his duties as lawman had consisted of handling a few drunks, keeping the drifters from hanging around overly long and settling an occasional neighborhood argument that arose over some minor incident.

He'd be there, handy, nevertheless, just in the event Tom and the town ever needed him; it just might be smart to have Tom Sutton swear him in as a sort of special deputy, one not on the payroll of course—Kilborn and the rest of the council wouldn't go for that—but fix it up so's he'd have some legal authority in case his services became necessary on short order. He'd talk to Tom about that.

Raking the sorrel lightly with his blunted spurs, Luke Jones moved on down the street, riding slow and easy, nodding to his many acquaintances as he passed. Folks in Mimbres Crossing thought a lot of him, he realized, and he'd only become aware of that after he'd served notice he was quitting the job. They began showing their appreciation then—something they'd never taken time to do before that moment—and there were quite a few who tried to talk him out of it.

He'd thanked them all and turned a deaf ear to their pleas. He was too old to do the job effectively any longer and was smart enough to admit it. Membres Crossing needed a younger man, and by sheer good fortune they had a perfect replacement in Deputy Tom Sutton.

There were some who did not share his trust in Tom, basing their convictions no doubt on what they knew of his father. Dave Sutton had been a drunk, a shiftless no-account, there was no denying that, but what folks didn't know was what had made him that way. All they saw was the man himself, cadging drinks from strangers or lying drunk somewhere in an alley or along the street. None of them ever knew what was inside the man.

Luke hadn't known either for a long time. Tom Sutton simply wouldn't talk about Dave to anyone, but finally he had opened up one day after someone had passed a particularly offensive remark about his father, and the old lawman had gotten the story.

Tom's mother had died in a fire. Dave Sutton had been off working at his job, and Tom, only a boy at the time, was at school. Dave had come home to see the house in flames and hear the cries of his wife, trapped inside. Helpless, restrained by neighbors, he'd been forced to stand by until the screams within the house had ceased and there was nothing left of the place but ashes.

Dave Sutton had never been the same after the tragedy. He quit his job and with Tom tagging along, began to drift from town to town while finding solace only in a bottle of whiskey, and doing whatever work he could persuade someone to give him. The recollection of the fire never left him and many times, Tom said, Dave had screamed out while asleep, calling to the agonized, dying woman trapped in the flames, that he was coming.

Those who were judging Tom Sutton by his pa didn't realize that Dave Sutton had once been a man much different from the one they knew, that Tom was like the person, steady and reliable, who existed before the fire had destroyed not only the woman he apparently loved very deeply but himself as well.

These facts Tom would not relate, nor would he permit Luke to repeat them and set Jess Fallon and Jergenson and the others who had their doubts about him, straight. They would take him for what he was, Tom had declared, and exacted a promise from Luke Jones to keep all he'd been told to himself. It would all come out some day, the old lawman guessed, and then Karl Jergenson and a few others would have to eat a lot of crow.

Luke reached the end of the street and once more hesitated, the question now arising in his mind as to whether he should go first and have his talk with Olive Bain about holding her classes in the school or at one of the girl's homes where there would be no question of safety, or ride on to the Evans place, five miles ahead on the road and open up the ditch and start the watering he planned to do. That might take a little time, especially if Mulehead Creek was low, and the teacher and her girls could be gone —and he wanted to have his words with them while they were there on the spot and he could point out the danger they were courting.

He'd swing by the picnic grounds first. It was more or less on the way to the Evans homestead. Then, after he'd gotten that little chore done, he'd go on and do his watering.

Again roweling the sorrel gently, Luke Jones turned off the street, and cutting in between two of the houses that stood on the east side, pointed for the grove.

5

J.J. waited while Deke Harvey and the other two men moved quietly into their assigned positions in the brush. When all were in place he drew himself upright, and utterly calm, walked boldly into the open.

The girls were sitting on a wool lap robe spread on the ground, their backs to him. The teacher, reading from a book, glanced up at the sound of Levitt's approach. A frown puckered her features.

"Morning," he said genially.

The teacher's frown deepened to a look of concern. "Good morning," she replied in a quiet, careful way.

The girls had all turned and were now facing Levitt. Halting before them, a hard smile on his lips, he nodded and raised a hand.

"All right, boys—"

Kirk, Harvey and Rufe Pearce stepped out of the brush. Immediately the teacher and all five of the girls came to their feet, fear mounting in their eyes.

"Just you stand nice and quiet," Levitt said in a firm, even voice. "Ain't none of you going to get hurt long as you do what you're told."

The teacher, surprise and shock gripping her tightly as the girls gathered around her, mustered a stern look.

"What do you want?" she demanded.

"You, missy," Rufe Pearce said, grinning as he and the

others closed in to form a circle around them. "All of you."

One of the girls began to weep. Levitt swept Pearce with a cold glance, then nodded reassuringly to the teacher and her charges.

"You ain't going to get hurt. Done told you that—and I keep my word. Rufe, there, ain't running this show, I am."

"What are you going to do?" the teacher asked, her voice trembling despite Levitt's words. "What do you want?"

"Money," J.J. said bluntly. "Aim to do some collecting from your pas."

The teacher frowned. "Kidnap us—hold us all for ransom?"

"Reckon that's how you'd say it—"

"You're wasting your time. My father—"

"Not thinking about your pa—it's them girls of your'n."

The young woman extended her arms, encircling her brood protectively. "You're going to make a lot of trouble for yourselves if you try it!" she warned. "The fathers of these girls are all important, influential men. They'll—"

"They won't be doing nothing except what I tell them to do," Levitt cut in coolly. "Now, we're going to gag and tie up the lot of you so's you won't kick up a ruckus, then we're going over to the schoolhouse and do some dealing and waiting. I'm sort of hoping we can do it all without no fuss because I don't want none of you getting hurt—but that's just what'll happen if any of you tries something. . . . Teacher, maybe you best make them understand that."

The young woman gave Levitt's words thought and glanced about at the girls. "Do just what they tell you."

One of the weeping girls began to sob harder. "Miss Bain, I—I—"

"It's all right, Charity," the teacher said soothingly. "Everything will be all right."

"Bain—that what you're called?" Levitt asked, as the other outlaws, at his sign, stepped in close and began to draw strips of cloth across the girls' lips and bind their wrists together behind them.

"Yes, I'm Olive Bain—and this—this tying and gagging us won't be necessary. The girls won't cause you any trouble."

"Maybe not," Levitt said, "but I ain't much of a hand to take chances. . . . There anybody at the schoolhouse this morning?"

Olive Bain shook her head, coming half about as Rufe Pearce roughly pulled her arms together and began to tie them.

"Ain't there somebody that does the cleaning up on Saturdays?" Levitt asked suspiciously.

"Well, yes, but I expect he's gone by now," the teacher said, looking down. "I never thought about—"

Levitt spat. "Just what I figured—you'll be trying to hornswoggle me if you get a chance. Reason I ain't about to make it easy for you to—"

Abruptly one of the girls, a tall blonde with clear blue eyes, whirled, broke away and darted into the brush. Levitt paused, swore softly, then made an impatient gesture at Deke Harvey.

"Go get her, kid."

The young outlaw wheeled, rushing off into the heavy undergrowth. Pearce, in the act of putting a gag on Olive Bain, grinned broadly.

33

"Should've let me go after that one, Levitt. I'd a sure cured her of trying to run off."

J.J. ignored the outlaw, settling his hard gaze on the teacher. "Seems I recollect you saying there weren't no need for tying and gagging—"

Olive struggled to avoid the strip of rag Rufe Pearce was endeavoring to affix. "Katie was just frightened."

"I don't give a damn what she was, lady! I was trying to be nice, but that ends right now. Next one to try running'll sure wish she hadn't!"

Olive jerked away from Pearce again. "They won't—I promise. Just leave this gag off my mouth so I can talk to them."

Levitt gave that brief thought and waved Rufe Pearce away. "All right, but you sure'n hell better not cross me. Way things've been going for me lately, I'm plumb out of patience, and I don't aim to let nobody spoil this here deal for me."

J.J. turned as Deke Harvey, pushing the tall girl called Katie ahead of him, broke out of the brush into the clearing. The girl, bits of leaves and twigs clinging to the front of her dress, a scratch on the side of her face, had evidently fallen in her attempted flight.

Olive Bain studied her anxiously. "Are you hurt?"

Katie shook her head, saying something unintelligible into her gag. The teacher, frowning, faced the others.

"We must all do exactly what we're told," she said. "You can see that it's useless to try and escape—and I have the promise of the man who seems to be the leader that no harm will come to us if we obey him."

Olive paused, centering her attention on a small, attractive girl with dark hair and eyes who was facing Deke Harvey.

34

The Proving Gun

"Amy Starr—are you listening to me?" she said sternly.

The girl whirled and bobbed hurriedly. The teacher continued to study her thoughtfully, her glance touching also Deke Harvey. Finally, she continued.

"We're being taken to the schoolhouse. There I assume your gags will be removed and the cords taken off your wrists—"

Levitt nodded. "Long as they don't try nothing."

"They won't. I'm giving you my word on that and I'll keep it—just as I expect you to stand by your promise that neither you nor any of your men will harm us."

"Ain't never broke my word yet," Levitt grumbled.

"Nor have I," Olive Bain retorted crisply. She glanced at each of the girls. "Do you all understand?"

All replied with nod. The teacher turned to Levitt. "We're ready."

He favored her with a hard, half smile as if faintly amused by her authoritativeness. He motioned to Harvey. "Get the surrey, boy. Best tie your horse on behind."

The younger man moved off to do Levitt's bidding. Rufe, arms folded across his chest, considered the girls and their teacher. He cocked his head at Kirk, standing beside him.

"Sure is a mighty pretty sight, ain't it?" he said, jabbing the smaller man with an elbow. "Was you to get your choosings, which one would you take?"

"Bring up the horses," Levitt snapped before Kirk could reply. "And Rufe, you keep your mind on what we're doing."

Pearce's dark features reflected anger for a brief moment, and then he wheeled and swaggered off into the brush.

Levitt shifted his attention to Olive Bain. "I'll be need-

35

ing their names," he said, jerking a thumb at the girls. "Might as well tell me now while we're waiting."

The teacher, eyes thoughtful and wary, also on Rufe Pearce, turned back to her charges. "Katie Jergenson"— she began looking at the tall blonde who had made the unsuccessful try at escaping—"next to her is Dulcie Henshaw, and then Amy Starr, Charity Maxwell and Lucy Teague."

Levitt smiled in satisfaction. "Come from real, high and mighty folks, near as I recollect. Sure don't figure I'll have trouble collecting plenty for them."

"I wouldn't know," Olive said coldly, and swung about to meet the surrey moving up beside them.

"Get aboard," Levitt ordered, again seemingly irked by the teacher's manner. "And keep remembering you'd best behave."

Amy Starr was the first into the vehicle, taking a seat beside Deke Harvey. The others, assisted by Levitt and Al Kirk, filled the remaining places—four on the rear seat and two in the front with the young outlaw.

"Mite crowded, I reckon," Levitt said, picking up the lap robe and tossing it onto the floor, "but we ain't going far." He turned to Pearce, riding up leading two horses, and swung onto the black gelding that halted beside him. He waved a hand at Harvey.

"You follow me. Al and Rufe'll trail along behind the surrey and keep watch—just in case somebody comes along and gets nosy—"

"Somebody has," Al Kirk broke in quietly, and pointed toward the trees to their right. A horse and rider were emerging from the shadowy depths of the grove.

Levitt flung a warning glance at Olive Bain. "Keep your

trap shut!" he snapped and spurred up close to Harvey. "Move out—slow, like you ain't in no hurry."

"Ain't fooling him, whoever he is," Pearce said. "He can see them gags." Abruptly the outlaw stiffened on his saddle. "Hell—it's the sheriff!"

"You—over there, what's going on?" the lawman called out, pulling to a stop.

"None of your goddam business!" Rufe Pearce shouted back.

"Aim to make it my business. You all just hold up there—"

"The hell with you!" Pearce replied, and whipping up his pistol, shot the lawman from his saddle.

For a long moment a stunned silence lay over the clearing, and then as muffled screams came from the girls, Levitt wheeled angrily to Pearce.

"You trigger-happy bastard!" he yelled through the thin cloud of powder smoke. "You've done it now for sure! Half the town'll have heard that shot and be down on us fast!"

"I wasn't about to let no tin star horn in on us," Pearce replied calmly, holstering his weapon. "It was you that said we had to make things work this time."

"I said that there wasn't to be no shooting and killing too!" Levitt snarled as he wheeled off in pursuit of the surrey.

6

The combination of a shoe coming loose from the hoof as well as a small stone lodged in the frog was all that troubled his horse, Sutton discovered. Bill McCandless, tall, lean and with sixty hard winters and summers behind him, had quickly removed the pebble with a hoof pick, and then summoning the young Mexican he employed as a stableboy, sent the bay gelding over to a nearby blacksmith for a pair of new shoes.

"Ain't right putting new iron on one side and not putting it on the other," the livery stableman declared. "Sort of throws the animal off balance—like a man trying to walk with one boot heel higher'n the other."

The explanation was unnecessary insofar as Tom was concerned, but he made no comment.

"Expect you're chomping at the bit waiting for Luke Jones to quit so's you can take over," McCandless continued as they walked slowly toward the double-door entrance to the sprawling, shadow-filled barn.

"Won't deny that," Sutton agreed.

"Reckon he's just as anxious to pass it all to you, too. He sure is looking ahead to settling down on that piece of ground he's got. Going out there again today, so he said."

Tom nodded. "I think he'd pin his star on me right today if he was dead certain I could handle the job."

McCandless drew a plug of tobacco from a pocket in his

stained overalls, gnawed off a corner. "Ain't him so much as it is Jergenson and some others. They're the ones that ain't sure."

Reaching the doorway, they halted. Sutton leaned a shoulder against the thick timber framework and glanced down the street.

"Don't know what I can do to make them feel any better about it," he said resignedly.

McCandless, working on his cud, shifted it to one cheek and spat into the loose dust. "Well, don't go losing no sleep on account of it. Always be people like Karl Jergenson around. Never satisfied with something, no matter what. Just got to be agin whatever it is other folks are for. . . . 'Cepting for him and Jess Fallon and maybe a half a dozen others, people around here are going to take Luke's word for you."

Two women came out of Miss Nickerson's shop on the opposite side of the street, paused briefly on the board sidewalk and then turned into the Rosebud Cafe, the adjoining building. McCandless drew a turnip-size, nickeled watch from the slit pocket in his overalls.

"Getting on to about dinnertime at that! Reckon my old woman's about got something ready. Care to join me?"

Sutton—tall, a bit too thin, with dark hair and eyes and features that caused him to appear older than his actual years—smiled, and shook his head.

"Obliged, Bill, but I'll pass. Didn't get around to eating breakfast until late. Appreciate the offer, however."

"Welcome now, welcome any time," McCandless said, and stepped out into the sunshine.

Sutton watched the older man shamble off toward the scatter of houses lying just west of the town for a few moments and then moved out into the open himself, pointing for the jail at the opposite end of the row of buildings.

Walking slow, he glanced into the shops as he passed, speaking to those who noted his passage, touching the brim of his hat in polite greeting to women, smiling to a small boy who burst suddenly from the passageway separating the bank and the General Store as he hurried to complete some errand upon which he'd undoubtedly been dispatched.

The hard, dry crack of a gunshot split the warm quiet. Sutton drew up abruptly, a frown pulling at his face. The report had come from the direction of the picnic grounds, and while someone firing off a weapon along the outskirts of the settlement was no novelty, the fact that the report had come from the grove where Luke Jones was headed brought a quick worry to the deputy.

He stood for a long minute listening, waiting, noting as he did that others along the street had also heard the shot and were pausing to stare off toward the south. Shortly Karl Jergenson, a large, raw-boned, blond man wearing an apron and with a pencil behind an ear, came out onto the landing fronting his store.

"That a gunshot I heard?" he wondered, the creases of his broad face deepening.

"What it sounded like. Came from the grove, I figure," Sutton replied.

"The grove?" Jergenson echoed. "My girl's over there—along with them others and the schoolteacher—"

"Sheriff's there too," Tom said, pivoting on a heel. "Like as not it was him shooting a rattler, or maybe a skunk, but I'll get my horse and have a look."

Jergenson made a comment of some sort but Sutton did not bother to listen, simply hurrying on back to the livery stable. As he turned into the runway he remembered his bay was at the blacksmith's, and his step was hastened by the worry that for some unaccountable reason was growing within him. He continued on to the corral off the rear of the barn where McCandless kept his stock of rental horses. Selecting the nearest, he threw on the necessary gear, mounted and cutting directly across the street, angled past the Poor Man's Saloon and turned toward the grove three miles below the town.

Holding his spurs to the little buckskin he was riding, Sutton reached the stand of trees and brush and swung into it. Moments later, as he broke out into the clear he saw the sheriff's sorrel gelding off to his left grazing contentedly on the thin grass that covered the area. There was no sign of Luke Jones, however, nor of Olive Bain and her girls or of the surrey.

Taut, Sutton rode directly toward the sorrel. The gelding paused in his cropping, raised his head and looked around. At that moment Tom saw the sprawled figure of the lawman, partly hidden by a clump of rabbit brush nearby.

Rushing in close, Sutton left the saddle in a long jump and crouched beside the prone shape. A broad stain of blood covered the lawman's chest. He was barely alive. Rising, Sutton glanced around. There was no one else in the grove—at least no one who was visible. Whoever had shot Luke was gone.

Wheeling, Sutton caught up the buckskin's reins and led him in to the lawman's side. Luke was in no condition to stay on a horse alone, and hanging him across a saddle would certainly be a fatal mistake. He'd have to ride double with the wounded man, holding him upright for the return to town.

Reaching down Tom lifted the sheriff's slight figure and

placed him on the saddle. Steadying the limp form, he swung up behind, and arm encircling Luke, Sutton headed back for the settlement. He'd send someone for Luke's horse. Important thing now was to get the old lawman to Doc Kenneman where he could receive treatment.

Once that was done he'd double back to the grove and the scene of the shooting, see if he could figure out what had happened, and try to run down whoever it was that had put a bullet in the sheriff. The bushwhacker couldn't have gotten far in so short a time—and there would be tracks.

Too, he'd best be sure everything was all right with Olive and the girls she'd had with her. Like as not the class had broken up and they had all returned to their homes, but he wanted to be certain of that; it was just possible there was some connection between Luke Jones being shot and their early absence from the grove.

Sutton reached the street and swung into it. He looked down at the sagging head of the man he was supporting, endeavoring to see the face. From behind, as he was, he could get only a restricted view, unable to tell if the lawman had recovered consciousness or not—or, possibly, was dead. Luke's body seemed lifeless.

A yell went up as he came into sight and slanted toward the hitchrack in front of the town's physician. Someone had noticed the arrival, and the word passed quickly. People began to appear in doorways, on store landings, at windows, and shortly a crowd was gravitating hurriedly toward Kenneman's quarters.

"What happened, Deputy?"

"Who shot him?"

"Is he dead?"

Tom shook his head at those and the growing barrage of

42

other questions thrown at him. Halting at the rack, he motioned to the nearest of several men.

"Give me a hand—"

Two stepped forward instantly to the side of the buckskin, and reaching up, pulled the old lawman off the saddle. Kenneman, framed in his doorway, his slack features emotionless as always, hesitated slightly and then came out onto his porch.

"Carry him in here," he ordered crisply, holding the screen open, and then leveled his small, black eyes on Sutton. "What happened?"

Tom pulled himself forward into the saddle. "I don't know," he said tightly. "You ask him when he comes to. I'm heading back there now, see what I can find out."

7

Luke Jones's sorrel had scarcely moved and was still grazing quietly when Sutton rode back into the cleared area of the grove. Drawing to a halt nearby, Tom sat for a time studying the ground and listening for any noises that might have meaning.

Not too much time had elapsed since he'd heard the gunshot and it was entirely possible the bushwhacker was yet in the grove; but that was a slim hope, Tom knew. Odds were that whoever it was had hurried off immediately after seeing the lawman fall from his saddle.

Who could it have been? No doubt Luke had enemies—a lawman could not do his job without incurring the ill will or outright hatred of a few, and Luke Jones had worn a badge for many years. It could be someone from the past, someone carrying a festering grudge and finally settling it. That it was someone living in Mimbres Crossing was also a possibility although it seemed unlikely.

Sutton's thoughts came to a halt, his mind going back to a short time earlier when Luke Jones and he had been standing in front of the jail idly discussing the future. A man had come from Abe Gilmer's Poor Man's Saloon—a stranger who had caught and held the lawman's attention. The sheriff had said that he did not recognize the man but his appearance had seemed to disturb him; could Luke have had a feeling—a hunch about the man? Was he the bushwhacker?

Coming off the saddle Tom began a close examination of the ground near where he had found the sheriff. After a few minutes he gave it up. No man riding or on foot had been near Luke when the bullet was fired. There were only the tracks of the lawman's sorrel leading out of the trees and halting at the edge of the clearing. Luke Jones had been shot from a distance.

Leading his horse, Sutton moved slowly on, working toward a central area where tables and benches, used by the people of the settlement at such times as Independence Day and other holidays, had been built. At once he came upon the wheel marks of the surrey Olive Bain and her girl students had been driving and the trampled bit of earth where the team of blacks that pulled it, had waited.

There was nothing unusual there, he decided; the surrey had entered the grove, its trail plain, and then departed, going south. That it was not returning to the schoolhouse was to be expected, as Charity Maxwell, whose father was the owner of the surrey, likely would swing by all of the girls' homes, dropping them off one by one before she returned to her own parents' residence.

But there appeared to be more hoofprints than would have been made by the team of blacks. That occurred to Sutton as he started to turn away, and pausing, he moved back to where the surrey had been standing. The ground was hard but there were impressions to be seen—the sharp cut of the shoes on the team, evidently new iron or almost so, and then the more difficult to see imprints of another horse that had stood behind the vehicle.

Someone had dropped by while Olive and the girls were there, and then when they departed, had tied his mount on behind the surrey. . . . Or it could have been another student, one of Olive's pupils arriving late for the Saturday morning session.

Continuing on, Tom followed the tracks of the surrey as it crossed the clearing. He halted again when he noted the point where a second horse had swung in beside the vehicle on its left while two more riders had come in from the right to join the party. All had then moved toward the lower end of the grove.

Make sure you're thinking straight. Things ain't always the way they seem.

Tom recalled Luke Jones's cautioning advice. But there was no reason to think there was a connection between Olive Bain and the girls and the shooting of Luke Jones. The riders who had united with the teacher and her class could have been other members, or they could have been boys from the school. . . . Best he keep searching about for other, more meaningful signs.

Doubling back, Sutton explored the area once more, going over it slowly and carefully, but the hard-packed ground revealed nothing more than he already knew; the girls and Olive had gathered in the usual place. When they were leaving four riders had joined them and all had departed together. There was nothing out of the ordinary about that and the only thing that disturbed Tom Sutton was his inability to find where the visitors had come in from, the brush fringing the picnic area being so dense and the ground so littered with dead leaves, twigs and other trash that there was no visible sign.

Perhaps it would be wise to return to town, recruit old Asa Williams, who'd lived in the mountains during the early days and claimed to be an expert tracker; Sutton gave that consideration, and then recalled Luke Jones's reaction to a similar suggestion he'd made one day when he and the lawman were searching for a strayed or stolen horse.

"Hell, Asa Williams couldn't find the cookshack," the sheriff had declared scornfully. "We do our own tracking, and if you figure you don't know much about doing it, here's your chance to learn first hand."

Tom smiled tightly at the recollection of the lawman's words and was grateful for them. They had gone on together, and with Luke pointing the way, calling attention to the many otherwise unnoticed signs and clues that made the trail clear, had successfully trailed the missing horse—and the drifter who had appropriated it.

It could be just as he figured, anyway. Olive and the girls had simply been joined by friends and then returned to their homes. Lucy Teague was one of those present and the Teague farm lay to the south of town. Likely Lucy was the first of the party to be delivered after which Charity Maxwell would drive on to the residences of the other girls.

Tom, clearly at a dead end, turned to the buckskin. There seemed to be no point wasting any more time in the grove; he had come up with no bit of evidence that would lead to the person, or persons who had shot Luke Jones. His best bet now was to return to town, see if the old lawman had regained consciousness and could name the bushwhacker.

Swinging into the saddle, Sutton started back across the clearing, and then on impulse, he cut around, reversing his course and rode onto the narrow tracks left by the Maxwell surrey. He'd follow them for a ways, be sure he was right; taking a few more minutes getting back to the settlement would make no difference.

The surrey, accompanied by the three riders, and with the fourth extra horse either tied to its rear or also being ridden, continued on through the grove following the well-beaten path of other vehicles, and finally broke out onto the flat lying beyond the tree-shaded area.

There it angled—not for the Teague place which was farther south—but to the bridge that spanned Mulehead Creek. Hesitating there, Tom puzzled over that realization and came to the conclusion that Lucy Teague was not being taken home first as he'd surmised, but was going on with the others. Apparently she intended spending the day with one of the girls.

Sutton rode on, crossing the flat strip of thick planks that echoed hollowly under the hoofs of the buckskin, and gained the opposite side. Here the surrey with its accompanying riders, had veered onto the main road and immediately all tracks melted into the myriad of prints left by previous passers-by. Determining which were old and which were freshly made was an impossibility.

But the party had headed back toward town, and it was now Tom's guess they were returning to the schoolhouse. Such was borne out by the fact that Lucy Teague had not been delivered to her home. Evidently Olive had further plans for her pupils and their visitors that morning, something that would be conducted at the schoolhouse. Too, the teacher could have heeded Luke Jones's advice and was forsaking the picnic grove, but Tom doubted there'd been time enough for the old lawman to talk with Olive. The gunshot had sounded shortly after he'd seen Luke ride out of town.

Abandoning the established route, Sutton cut directly across the flat, loping the buckskin steadily for the squat, solidly built structure where Olive Bain held classes.

There he would find her and the girls and whoever their visitors were, he was certain; it was only logical. But there was an uneasiness stirring within Tom Sutton where the teacher and her pupils were concerned, one he knew could be dispelled only by making sure.

Maybe he was handling the situation wrong, he thought as the buckskin hurried over the grassy lifts and falls, but he could think of no other way to go about it. How would Luke Jones have faced the situation? Could the old lawman have done any more than he was doing?

It was a strange twist of fate. He had planned to rely heavily upon Luke for help and advice, and the very first time it was needed, the lawman was in no position to give it. Instead he was being forced to depend upon himself; he could only hope he was following the right course.

The schoolhouse, its gray, blocky shape standing bleak in the sunlight, was just ahead. Sutton pulled the buckskin down to a walk, a frown clouding his features. The surrey was not there. It should be drawn up to the hitchrack at the side of the building, the one provided for the pupils of the outlying area who rode to school on horseback or in buggies and buckboards or other types of vehicles.

Nor was there any indication of someone in or around the structure. With its doors shut, shades pulled over the windows, the barns and sheds to the rear all closed, the school was as it should be on a Saturday—completely deserted. Olive and the others had evidently gone somewhere else, to one of the girl's homes, or on a picnic, perhaps.

Sutton swore impatiently. Hell, there were a dozen things he could come up with to explain the absence and whereabouts of Olive Bain and the girls—any one of which could be right.

The Proving Gun

He was only losing time trying to guess where they were —and there was no real indication they were involved in the shooting of Luke Jones. The smart thing to do was return to town, talk to the old lawman. Then he would have the answers he needed. Cutting the buckskin about, Tom headed for the settlement at a fast run.

8

"The sheriff never regained consciousness," Doc Kenneman said. "Fact is, he was all but gone when you brought him in."

Tom wheeled slowly away from the sheet-covered figure of the lawman lying on the metal and wood examining table in the physician's office and met the questioning gaze of the dozen or so men crowding the room. He knew without their asking what they wanted to know.

"I couldn't find any signs of who shot Luke," he said heavily. "Hunted around good. Only tracks were those of Olive Bain and her girls, and somebody that dropped by, visiting—probably boys from her class."

"That where it happened—there at the picnic grounds?" Kilborn asked.

Tom nodded to the town's mayor. "He was laying near the edge of the trees. Whoever it was shot him as he rode into the clearing."

"Damned odd you couldn't find no sign," Jergenson said impatiently. "One man just can't ride up to another, shoot him and then ride off without leaving some kind of a trace. You sure you didn't miss something?"

The skepticism in the storekeeper's voice was unmistakable. Anger stirred through Tom Sutton, and then he pressed it back. There were those who had doubts concerning his ability to handle Luke Jones's job, and chief among them was Karl Jergenson; he'd known that all along. There was no sense in letting it rile him now.

"Like I said, only tracks I could turn up were those of the surrey—your surrey I think it was, Maxwell—and of some riders, boy friends of the girls, I figured, who joined Olive and her party when they left."

"I take it the girls had already gone then when you got there," the banker said, frowning.

"Yes—was nobody around at all. . . . Reckon the best thing we can do now is mount a posse and start to combing the country. Whoever it was hasn't had time enough to get far."

"Where'll you commence? You don't even know what direction to look into," Jergenson said, shrugging. "Take a hell of a lot of men—"

"I know that," Tom said coldly.

"What about those riders you say joined up with the girls?" Maxwell wondered, continuing his line of questioning. The frown on his face had deepened to one of worry. "I don't recollect seeing any of the boys around town heading out that way. What makes you sure that's who they were?"

"I'm not sure—only guessing."

"Guessing!" Jergenson exploded. "That's a hell of a way to do something. You ought've made certain."

"How could he?" Kenneman cut in dryly. "Man said they were gone when he got there. Assuming that's the way it was is all he could do."

"By God, he could've followed—"

"I did," Tom said quietly, "after I went back."

"That would've been fifteen, twenty minutes later," Jess Fallon said. "Trail was already getting cold and they'd been out of sight. Might've been smarter to've taken off after them right at first."

"The sheriff was still alive. I wanted to get him to Doc as quick as I could."

"Well, I'm still thinking about my daughter and those other girls," Maxwell said, shaking his head. "It occurs to me that I haven't seen Charity or any of the others and they're usually back from those Saturday morning outings by now."

"Tracked the surrey to the Mulehead Creek bridge. They turned onto the road there, headed back towards town. I supposed they were going to the schoolhouse."

"That what they did?"

"Didn't see any sign of them when I got there so I figured then they must've gone on home, or maybe somewheres else to hold class. Luke aimed to talk to Olive, tell her—"

"Figured!" Jergenson said, again in a loud, exasperated way. "Don't you know anything for sure, Deputy?"

"Ease off, Karl," Huffman said, gesturing at the storekeeper. "Boy done what he thought was right."

Temper lifted within Sutton once more. Most of the men were looking upon him as if he'd done something wrong, had failed them.

"What the hell else could I have done?" he demanded, anger finally boiling over. "Mind telling me how you would've handled it?"

"I sure as the devil wouldn't've just guessed at everything the way you done!" Jergenson snapped.

"That mean you would've left the sheriff laying there bleeding to death while you went hunting for them?"

It was Bill McCandless. The stableman pointed a gnarled finger at the owner of the General Store and wagged his head. "You wouldn't've done no different, Karl, and you damn well know it! Sutton didn't have no choice. But—with all this jawing—we're wasting time if we're going to get a posse together."

"Seems to me we ought to find out first if the girls are all right," Henry Maxwell said. "I think those of us who had daughters out there with that teacher had best send word to our homes, see if they're safe. Anybody know who was in the party?"

"Your daughter, the Henshaw girl, Amy Starr, Katie Jergenson and Lucy Teague," Sutton replied. "Luke and I saw them when they drove out of town. I started to mention earlier that the reason Luke rode over to the grove was because he wanted to have a talk with Olive, warn her about holding her class there. He was afraid some day a drifter might bother them."

"That'd be Luke Jones—always thinking ahead, looking out for the folks in town," Fallon murmured. "Sure going to miss him."

Henry Maxwell brushed nervously at his jaw. "Them going out there always worried me some too—"

"Same here," Jergenson agreed, his belligerent manner now changing to one of concern.

"Think I'll walk over to the house, see if Charity's there," the banker continued, turning away.

"Don't see your surrey out front," someone offered, glancing through the window.

"Could be around back. . . . Karl, you'd best get in touch with your wife too. Be a good idea for somebody to ride over to the Teagues, the Henshaws and the Starrs while we're gone and see if the girls are there. Could save us some time if—"

Henry Maxwell's voice broke and he didn't finish as he

moved toward the door. Kilborn cleared his throat noisily.

"Meanwhile, we better let the deputy get his posse together. We'll be needing it either way it turns out."

The banker nodded, and followed by Jergenson and the others, continued for the exit. They halted abruptly as Clell Adams appeared before them on the porch. The gun-shop owner, in company with a small boy carrying a folded sheet of paper in his hand. Adams glanced about, settling his attention on John Kilborn.

"Kid here's got a note for you, Mayor. Says some men up at the schoolhouse told him to fetch it to you."

"Note?" Kilborn repeated, pushing forward. Taking the paper from the youngster, he opened it, scanned it briefly, glanced at Maxwell and then to Jergenson.

"Concerns you, Henry, you too, Karl."

The banker's features tightened and Jergenson's shoulders came up stiffly.

"What do you mean?" the storekeeper asked in a cautious sort of tone.

"Your girls—and the others. They're being held for ransom."

A stunned silence fell over the room. Henry Maxwell let out a long sigh.

"God in heaven—who by?"

"Don't say. Letter was written by the teacher and there's only her signature and words below it saying she was told to write it. They want ten thousand dollars from each of you, and from Teague, Ben Starr and Vic Henshaw. Fifty thousand in all—and they want it by dark."

"Fifty thousand!" Jergenson muttered in a strangled voice. "My God, there ain't that much loose cash in the whole county!"

"They say they'll kill them all if you don't kick through,"

Kilborn continued. "You're to send it to the schoolhouse. They're holed up there."

"Schoolhouse!" Fallon echoed, whirling to Sutton. "I thought you said you rode up there and looked around."

Tom nodded. "Place was closed up—leastwise it looked to be. There was nobody in sight, and there was no sign of Maxwell's surrey."

"You try the doors, look in the barn?"

"No. I figured—"

"You figured!" Karl Jergenson shouted. "That's all I've heard from you—figuring and guessing! If you'd had the sense to—"

"What difference would it have made?" Kenneman broke in with a wave of his hand. "You'd have only got the word sooner. Question now is what're you going to do about it? Way I see it those kidnapers, whoever they are—"

"Likely it's them riders the deputy was talking about—" Huffman offered.

"Probably—they're holding all the high cards."

"And I'm betting one of them killed the sheriff, too, when he tried to keep them from grabbing the girls," McCandless said. The stable owner shifted his attention to Tom Sutton. "You're mighty lucky you didn't stop a bullet yourself, riding up to that schoolhouse the way you done."

"If he did," Jergenson said in a low voice and again started for the door.

Anger surged through Sutton. He stepped forward, caught the storekeeper by the arm and jerked him around.

"I went there," he said coldly. "I'm admitting I didn't go in. There was no reason to. I was looking for the surrey and the horses. When I didn't see it—"

"You figured there wasn't nobody around," Jergenson finished, pulling free. "Thing you best learn, boy, if you aim to make a lawman, is to be sure about things and stop figuring."

Sutton's face colored as anger once more rushed through him. He had done what he thought was the right thing but Jergenson, and probably some of the others, were criticizing him for it. What the hell else did they expect of him? He'd had no way of knowing the four riders that had joined Olive Bain's party were outlaws and that they had kidnaped her and the girls!

Shrugging, Tom stepped back. Let it pass. That's what Luke Jones would do if he were standing in his boots at that moment. It might have been better had he dismounted and gone up to the schoolhouse to make certain but it would have made no difference in the end, as Doc Kenneman had pointed out—except for one thing; had he made a close examination of the premises and been taken captive during the process, his presence might then have served as a deterrent to the outlaws and prevented any possible harm from coming to Olive and the girls—assuming, of course, the renegades hadn't killed him.

McCandless stirred restlessly. "We ought to be doing something. Standing here arguing's a waste of time."

Jed Huffman nodded. "Seems to me it's up to Maxwell and Jergenson and the others as to whether they're going to pay the ransom or not—"

"Whether!" the banker said bitterly. "We don't have a choice—but raising that much, I'm not sure it can be done in the time they're giving us."

"We need to get word to Teague and them," Kilborn said.

Sutton, recalling some of Jones's advice, seized the moment to take charge. "I'll see to that," he said, and ignoring Jergenson, turned to the banker. "I'll need to know exactly what your plans are, Henry. I aim to ring this town with armed men to wait for that bunch when they ride out but I won't dare make a move until the girls are safe."

"Best you stick around close where we can find you," John Kilborn cautioned. "The note says for a deputy to deliver the cash soon as it's ready."

"The deputy," a voice in the crowd repeated. "Guess that's all the proof we need that they're the ones that shot down old Luke. They know he's dead."

Sutton glanced at the speaker. It was Pete Avery. Standing close by were his brother Gabe and their Kansas friend Buffalo Finch.

Kilborn considered Avery for a long moment. Then, "Don't go getting any ideas about taking matters into your own hands. Those outlaws are Sutton's business, and he'll tend to them after Henry Maxwell and the others have done what they have to do."

"Yeah, reckon he'll try, anyway," Avery said with a laugh. "But so far his guessing and figuring ain't been too good. I'd say he's needing plenty of help."

Tom nodded coldly to the man. "Could be, Pete," he said. "But don't hang around waiting. When and if that time comes you won't be the kind of help I'll be looking for."

9

Karl Jergenson flicked Sutton with a derisive glance, muttered something in a low voice and moved on for the door, Maxwell at his heels.

"I'll get word to Teague and Vic Henshaw and Ben Starr," he said, making it clear that he was unwilling to entrust the chore of dispatching messengers to the other families involved to anyone else. "We'll be meeting at Henry's bank in one hour, and seeing what we can do about raising the cash."

"I'll be there," Kilborn said. "Goes without saying you're welcome to use what money I've got laid by."

Kenneman and several others spoke up, making known their willingness to help also. Jergenson bobbed his head and Maxwell expressed his appreciation vocally, and both continued on to the street

Huffman cocked his head to face Tom Sutton. "That there posse you was talking about—you still want to mount it?"

"No need for it—yet," the young lawman replied. "No doubt in my mind that Luke's killer is one of the bunch that's holding Olive and the girls—"

"That a guess?" Gabe Avery asked, grinning broadly.

Sutton's jaw tightened but he hung onto his temper. Luke Jones had warned him there'd be times such as this—moments when his wisdom would be doubted and his judgment challenged. It was a strange thing, the old lawman had said, but folks expressed their confidence in a man by electing him to do a job for them, and then were prone to question the things he did to get that job done. It didn't exactly apply to him, Tom realized, since he hadn't been elected to office, but he was the only lawman in Mimbres Crossing and therefore in the same situation.

"Just do your own figuring out and decide what's right and what ought to be done," Luke had advised, "then go ahead."

"More than a guess," Tom said evenly, attention on the younger Avery. "Only tracks I could find were Luke's when he came into the clearing, and the ones made by four riders when they rode out with the surrey. Way I see it is that the sheriff showed up unexpectedly while they were leaving with the girls and one of them shot him."

"Makes sense," McCandless agreed, "but I reckon we'll know for sure once we get to talk to them girls and the teacher."

"If they're able to talk," Pete Avery murmured.

"What do you mean by that?" the livery stable owner demanded.

Avery shrugged. "That bunch didn't hold back on shooting down a sheriff, they ain't going to hold back doing whatever they want with them girls—kill them too, if they take the notion."

"Hell, excepting for the teacher, they ain't much more'n kids," Jed Huffman said.

"Won't make no difference to them. Long as they—"

"That's enough of that kind of talk," Kenneman cut in roughly. "It's money those men are after. The girls are just a means for getting it so don't go spreading ideas that'll make their folks worry all the more. Besides, we don't know that those men are the kind that would take advantage. I've met some outlaws who were gentlemen, and some so-called gentlemen who were swine."

"There any chance of me getting into that schoolhouse without them knowing it?" Sutton wondered.

"Not even a little one," McCandless replied. "I was in on fixing up the place after the town took it over. Old man Zimmerman built it like he was expecting all the Indians in the country to come down on him. Good as being inside a fort."

"One man could hold off a small army," Fallon agreed. "Windows are all high and small, and there's just two doors, and he could block one and stand watch at the other—and there's four of them, according to what you told us."

"Four that I'm certain of," Tom said. "Was three riding alongside the surrey, and a horse trailing along behind like he was tied to the back axle."

"They probably had one doing the driving."

The room was quiet for a long breath and then Kenneman hunched to his knees and faced the youngster who had brought the message.

"You're the Lewis boy, aren't you? Name's Norman?"

"Yes, sir—"

"How did it happen those men at the schoolhouse gave you that note for the mayor?"

The boy smiled, pleased to be the center of adult attention. "I was cutting across the yard, going to the store for ma. Then this man hollered at me from the door. I didn't pay him no mind at first, then Miss Bain come up and stood next to him. She said it was all right and I was to do what he told me. That's when he gave me that there letter and told me to take it to the mayor, real fast. And that's what I done."

"You see anybody else besides the teacher and that man?"

"Nope, just them."

"Did Miss Bain look like she was all right, or had she been hurt?"

"Looked just the same as she does every day in school."

The physician nodded, then patted the boy on the head. "You did fine, Norman," he said, rising. "Run along now and finish that errand your ma sent you on."

Still smiling, the boy turned and scurried out of the room. McCandless shrugged. "Reckon things was going all right up to then—leastwise, far as the teacher's concerned."

Kenneman nodded. "Fortunate thing Olive Bain's with those girls. She's a strong young woman and her being with them will keep them from falling apart."

"All depends on whether she's having troubles of her own or not," Huffman said.

Tom Sutton swore silently. He was regretting more and more his failure to check the schoolhouse, but there was nothing to be done about it—and getting inside now was apparently out of the question. He could only bide his time and hope for the best where Olive and the girls were concerned.

"You think Maxwell and them'll be able to pay the ransom?" McCandless asked.

"Anybody's guess," Kenneman said, "but fifty thousand dollars is a lot of money and I've got my doubts. It's the wrong time of the year. Everybody's low on cash. If this had happened in the fall after the cattle sales and the harvests, I'd say the chances would be good."

"Couldn't Henry Maxwell loan the others—"

"Depends on whether the bank's got that much cash on hand. I doubt that too."

"Then we best be making some plans about what we're going to do if they can't pay off," Pete Avery said. "I'm for rushing them—"

"We're going to leave that up to Henry Maxwell and the others," Sutton cut in quickly. "They're the ones with the most at stake."

"Can't see as they'll have much of a choice. Just have to risk those girls getting hurt. That bunch killed the sheriff and it ain't right to let them get away with it."

Pete Avery had suddenly become a very law-abiding citizen, Tom thought with a half smile. Most likely, however, it was the fever and excitement of becoming involved in such an occasion—like being in a lynch mob.

"They'll have to eat and they'll be needing water. We could just set back and starve them out," Gabe Avery suggested.

"Means starving the girls too," McCandless said scornfully. "You think of that?"

"Then what the hell're we going to do?"

"Wait, that's what," Sutton said quietly.

"Wait? Ain't going to get us nothing, waiting. Doc's already said Maxwell and them won't be able to pay the ransom—"

"I only said I had my doubts," the physician cut in. "I don't know the financial condition of any of them."

Jess Fallon sighed heavily. "Well, it's a hell of a mess. I sure wish Luke Jones was here, running things."

"He couldn't do any more than Sutton," Kenneman snapped. "Now, I want you all to get out of here. You can do your waiting somewhere else. I've got work to do. I'd be obliged if one of you'd drop by Overmier's and tell him to bring over a coffin."

"He's already here, waiting on the porch," someone volunteered.

The physician smiled wanly, murmured something and turned to the table where the body of Luke Jones lay. He hesitated briefly as the crowd began to file out, and then reaching under the sheet he'd drawn over the lawman, unpinned the star on the dead man's vest.

"Deputy—"

Sutton halted. Others nearby him also paused. "Yeh?"

"You might as well pin this on," the doctor said, handing Tom the badge. "You're the sheriff now."

Sutton took the star, studied it for a long moment. Then, removing the deputy insignia he was wearing, he replaced it with that of Luke Jones.

"Ain't sure that's legal," Jess Fallon said, rubbing at his jaw.

"Why isn't it?" Kenneman demanded irritably. "The sheriff's dead so the deputy takes his place."

"Seems the mayor and town council ought to meet—"

"Oh, for God's sake, Jess, don't get another fuss started!" the physician groaned. "Far as the town's concerned Sutton's now the sheriff. Would've been the first of the year, anyway—so what difference does a few months make?"

The saloon man was silent for a time and then his thick shoulders lifted and fell. "No, I reckon it won't make any difference. Sure would feel a heap better, however, if we had somebody with a bit more experience running things. From what I've seen so far I ain't so sure the boy can handle it."

Sutton grinned tightly. "I'd like for you to get one thing straight, Fallon—I'm no boy. I'm old enough to do my job, and I can! Now, when Maxwell and the others are ready for me, they'll find me in my office."

"Your office?" Pete Avery echoed in feigned surprise.

"You heard the sheriff," Bill McCandless said firmly, and followed Tom out of the doctor's quarters.

10

When the townspeople of Mimbres Crossing had remodeled the old Zimmerman place for use as a school, they had torn out the inside walls that divided the structure into four irregular-sized rooms and erected instead a single partition that created two large areas, one half of which Olive Bain utilized as quarters for the small children, the other for the older boys and girls. Now, with J. J. Levitt and his three outlaw companions in charge, all had gathered in the latter section.

Upon arriving at the schoolhouse, and after the surrey and horses were safely out of sight in the barn, Levitt had ordered the gags and the short lengths of rope removed, and with a curt wave of his hand, directed the girls to a back corner of the room. Olive complied immediately, instructing the girls to each draw up a chair and sit quietly facing the wall, warning them that under no circumstances were they to talk, smile or pay any attention to the men.

"The slightest bit of encouragement on your part will only lead to serious trouble," she had said.

The outlaws had prowled about inside the building for several minutes after entering, familiarizing themselves with its arrangement of exits and windows, and finally satisfied there was no possible way to enter except by the front and rear door, had settled down. Levitt and Al Kirk stationed themselves at the front while the one who had shot Sheriff Jones—Rufe—and Deke, the youngest of them positioned themselves at the rear.

Now, as she sat in the center of the girls grouped closely around her in their corner of the room and listened to the vague noises coming from the town a quarter mile in the distance, Olive wondered what lay in store for her and her charges.

The outlaws were desperate men, turned more so by the fact they had undoubtedly killed Luke Jones and faced not only kidnaping charges but one for murder as well. Thus it was only good, common sense to believe that the men would stop at nothing to gain their end.

The shooting of Sheriff Jones had been a mistake. J.J. had berated and cursed Rufe angrily for doing so, calling him a trigger-happy fool and a few other names that had set her and the girls to blushing in embarrassment, and for a moment or two Olive had thought the two men were going to have it out. But Rufe had finally shrugged and laughed it off, ending the tight moments.

There was little, if any, friendship between the two. Olive readily recognized that fact and guessed that someday there would come a settlement between them. Evidently they had worked together before in holdups or perhaps kidnapings, and this hadn't been the first time Rufe had complicated matters by using his pistol thoughtlessly.

But whatever personal problems the pair had was of no concern to her; protecting the five girls for whom she felt responsible, was. J.J. had assured her no harm would befall them when she wrote the note to Mayor Kilborn for him setting forth the terms of the ransom. All that was necessary was for the parents to pay, he'd said, and she and the girls would be all right.

Her hopes had soared at that point, only to plummet

when he quoted the amount of cash they wanted. Fifty thousand dollars! The fathers of the girls were all well off, she was aware of that, but ten thousand dollars each! Olive doubted very much that any of them possessed that much ready cash, and the outlaws were giving them little time to raise it. By sundown of that very day, that was the deadline, and already it was past noon. Making a trip to one of the larger towns where a loan or a mortgage might be arranged was simply out of the question.

There was some reason why J.J. and his outlaw friends were insisting the ransom be paid by dark, Olive realized. There had been no mention of it but she gathered it from the way the men had talked—some vague, indefinite reference to the past and a need to reach the border and cross over into Mexico as soon as possible.

What would happen to them if the families of the girls were able to pay the ransom and all of the provisions for a safe departure outlined by J. J. Levitt in the note were complied with? Would the outlaws still hold them hostage to guarantee their passage to the border?

She couldn't imagine Ben Starr, Amy's father, or Karl Jergenson, for that matter, standing by and letting the outlaws get away with all that money. Both were hardheaded and inclined to anger, and the very first thing they would do would be to set up a trap for the outlaws once their daughters were out of danger. The other men—Vic Henshaw and Henry Maxwell and Mr. Teague would join with them, of course, in making such a move.

And so would Tom Sutton. He was the town's lawman now that Luke Jones was shot, and he would be out to capture the outlaws not only for that crime but for the kidnapings as well. She wasn't sure if Tom could handle the responsibility that had descended so abruptly on his shoulders or not, and she knew she was not alone in harboring such doubts.

But Tom Sutton would try, would do his best; of that much Olive was absolutely certain, and she hoped he would prove himself capable of meeting the test since he was so determined to become a good lawman. However, his intentions to capture the outlaws, as well as those of the girls' fathers to intercept them would have to be forgotten if Levitt and the others decided to take along one or more hostages in order to guarantee safe passage—

"Miss Bain—"

At Lucy Teague's low-voiced words Olive glanced up. Rufe had deserted his post at the door and was standing just outside the half circle of chairs. He was grinning broadly at Katie Jergenson.

"You're sure a mighty fine-looking gal," the outlaw said, nodding his shaggy head.

His eyes were bloodshot and there were fragments of food trapped in the stubble of beard that covered the lower part of his face. The rank smell of the man, even from the six feet or so that separated him from the girls, was sickening.

"Whyn't me and you get ourselves a little better acquainted?" he rumbled thickly. Evidently he had been helping himself liberally to the near-empty bottle of liquor that was jammed into a hip pocket.

"Leave us alone," Olive said sternly.

Rufe's features hardened. "Ain't talking to you, Missy Schoolma'am. Talking to the gal with the pretty yellow hair."

J. J. Levitt rose slowly, crossed the full length of the room and halted near Rufe. His lined features were expressionless.

"Go set down," he said. "I told you these girls wasn't to be bothered. I meant it."

Rufe reached for the bottle to take another long swallow. "You ain't my pappy—and if you was I sure wouldn't pay you no mind. Nobody tells Rufe Pearce what to do."

J.J. drew up slowly, eyes narrowing. At that moment Deke stepped up, laying a hand on Pearce's arm.

"Come on, Rufe," he said coaxingly. "You never did finish telling me about that time down in Laredo when you took on all them Mexicans."

Pearce stirred. His sullen, fixed stare locked to J.J.'s stolid features broke and lowered. He turned to the younger man.

"Seems I recollect I did—"

"Nope, you didn't and I'd sure like to hear all about it."

Rufe came about, a sort of swagger in his motions, and started back toward the door. A quick grin parted Deke's lips as he glanced at Amy Starr and winked. Olive saw the girl return the smile, frowned and then nodded to J.J.

"Thank you," she murmured.

Levitt merely pivoted on a heel of his worn boot, and recrossed the room to where Al was hunched, shoulders to the wall.

Katie Jergenson began to weep quietly, raggedly. Olive reached forward and took the girl's hand in her own.

"It's all right. Don't be afraid."

"I—I can't help it," Katie sobbed. "The way he looks at me—I get cold chills. I just know he—"

"That Mr. Levitt won't let him bother you," Olive continued, "but we must be careful not to give him or any of them a reason to try and get friendly." She paused, placing her attention on Ben Starr's daughter. "That means you,

Amy! I've noticed the way you've been looking at Deke and smiling at him."

The girl tossed her head indifferently. She was small, pretty, had dark hair and eyes, and there was much of her father's independence in her.

"I think he's cute—"

"Cute!" Olive Bain gasped. "He's an outlaw, probably a murderer just like Rufe Pearce. You must be out of your mind to even think of him in that way!"

Katie Jergenson had ceased her weeping, and with the other girls, was listening intently, eyes on Amy. Elsewhere in the shadowy room Rufe Pearce was engaged in an animated recounting of his adventures to Deke while J.J. and Al appeared to be dozing. Off in the direction of town a dog was barking frantically at something that disturbed him.

Amy shrugged. "He doesn't seem to be like the others—and he's so young. I'll bet he's only a year or two older than I."

"That doesn't make any difference," Olive said sternly, keeping her voice to a firm whisper. "Getting friendly with him can only mean serious trouble for you. Now, I don't want to see you smiling at him again—or even looking in his direction. Do you understand?"

Amy Starr made no reply, only stared at her folded hands now resting in her lap. Olive shifted her attention to Katie. The Jergenson girl had begun to weep softly again.

"Do you think we'll get out of this alive?" Lucy Teague asked in her direct, matter-of-fact way.

"I'm sure of it," Olive replied.

"But it's been two hours at least since they sent that ransom note, and we haven't heard anything from it."

"That's to be expected. They're asking for a lot of

money. It will take time for your fathers to get that much together."

Lucy plucked at the hem of her dress. "Ten thousand dollars—I know Papa doesn't have that much cash."

"Neither does mine," Dulcie Henshaw said. "He just bought some more cattle. I heard him say he was cash broke and cow poor just the other day."

"I don't know about my father," Charity Maxwell said. "He may be a banker but that doesn't mean he has a lot of money. What's in a bank belongs to other people, mostly."

"In a case like this I expect everyone will pitch in and help," Olive said, striving to reassure the girls. "I doubt if any of your families can get together that much cash on such short notice."

There was a long silence after that, and then Lucy Teague asked the question Olive Bain knew was foremost in all their minds.

"What if they can't raise the ransom—even with others helping all they can? What will happen to us?"

Olive managed a smile. "We won't think about it that way. You all know what we've learned about the importance of looking at things in a positive manner. That's just what we must do now—believe firmly your fathers will manage it somehow."

"That's hard to do—"

"I know, but it's the same as having faith in something. Often it's difficult to maintain our beliefs, but we must, and if we do, things will all come out in the way we hope."

Olive hesitated, her glance moving to Amy Starr. The girl's eyes were reaching across the room to the young outlaw, Deke. A smile was on her lips.

"Amy!"

Immediately the girl looked away. Olive sighed wearily.

The Proving Gun

"I want you to exchange chairs with Lucy," she said, and waited while the switch was made. Then, "Thank you."

At least Amy Starr's back was now turned to Deke but whether that would stem the obvious attraction the young outlaw had aroused in Ben Starr's daughter was problematical.

73

11

Levitt looked up at the big, white-faced, black-numbered Regulator clock ticking hollowly on the wall above the schoolteacher's desk. . . . Seventeen minutes past three o'clock. . . . He swore deeply under his breath and brushed at the sweat accumulated on his forehead. Something should have happened by now; it had been four— almost five—hours since he'd sent that kid with the note to the town's mayor. It seemed to him they'd had plenty of time to get the money together.

Swiping again at his face, he glanced around the room. Rufe Pearson, whiskey finally having its way, was sprawled on the floor near the door, sleeping soundly. Close by Deke Harvey was idly spinning the cylinder of his pistol, hat pushed to the back of his head. In the adjacent corner the teacher had her girls gathered in a tight half circle of chairs facing inward while she maintained a watch over them, like a mother hen guarding her chicks from preying hawks. . . . She was a cool one, that Miss Olive Bain.

"What do you reckon's going on?" Al Kirk muttered, shifting his position on the hard floor in an effort to find a bit of comfort. "We ought to be hearing from somebody."

"Just what I've been thinking," Levitt replied. "Time's starting to run out."

"You figure they'll kick through?"

"Sure they will," Levitt said confidently. "We got them by the short hairs. Ain't no man going to let his kid get hurt —especially a girl—for a few dollars."

"Few!" Deke Harvey said, coming up at that moment. Evidently he, too, was beginning to worry at the delay. "Fifty thousand is one hell of a lot of dollars was you to ask me. You think we can get that much?"

Levitt's shoulders twitched. "Don't do no harm to ask for the top. Maybe they've got it, maybe they ain't. Point is they'll pay off what they can. . . . Always smart to start high when you're dickering, then come down if you have to. Easy to cut your price but hell to raise it."

"I'm starting to wonder if they're going to pay anything," Deke said disconsolately. "It looks to me like they're aiming to just let us set here, sweat it out. . . . All the same as being in jail."

"With night coming on and them girls with us? Not much they won't."

Deke half-turned to look at the girls and their teacher. Dropping to his haunches, he jerked a thumb in their direction.

"What about them, J.J.?"

"Well, what about them?"

"Once we get the money, what're you figuring on doing with them?"

"Turn them loose—all save the teacher."

"That ain't what Rufe's planning. He's got his mind set on having that yellow-haired gal—the one that tried to get away—"

"Rufe'll do what I say," Levitt cut coldly. "Nothing's happening to any of them kids. We lay a hand on any one of them and her pa'll see to it we never get ten miles out of town—no matter what it takes. Reason I'm picking the teacher to be the hostage. She's growed and there won't be no big fuss made over us taking her along."

"Could be we're sort of overlooking something," Al Kirk said, again changing position. "That there sheriff—Rufe killed him surer'n hell. They'll be wanting us for murder."

"That goddam fool of a Rufe," Levitt muttered harshly. "I should've expected him to mess things up again, but maybe it won't make no difference. It's the girls they'll all be thinking about—not that dead tin star, and once we're across the border we can forget about the killings Rufe's done."

"Maybe we ought to take a couple of them girls along with the teacher just to make it a cinch—"

"No, she'll be enough. Like I said we don't want any of their pas coming after us."

"Well, I'm sure going to be mighty glad when we're out of here," Kirk said, wagging his head. "Like the kid says, it's the same as being in the jug. Besides, I'm getting plenty hungry. We ain't hardly et in two days."

"You can fill your belly good once we're in Mexico. You'll have enough cash money in your pockets to buy yourself a whole storeful of grub, if that's what you want."

Kirk grunted. "All I'll be wanting when we get there is a square meal. After that I'll start thinking on what else I aim to do."

Deke pulled off his hat and scratched at his head. "Ain't decided yet what I'm doing with my share, either. Might just set out a spell down there, enjoy myself. Then when I get tired of that maybe I'll ride back over to Texas, buy myself a little spread and start raising cattle. . . . What're you figuring on, J.J.?"

The older man smiled grimly. "Boy, I've been around too long to count my chickens before the eggs is hatched—

but I sure won't end up raising cattle. Cows are the most aggravating critters God give life to. Plumb drive a man loony. Expect I'll just find me a place and settle down, watch the sun come up and set and not do no thinking or fretting about anything."

"About how I feel too," Kirk said. "Just plain doing nothing sounds right good to me, but like J.J. says, we best hold off making plans till we get the cash in our pockets. You think it'd be smart to send another note to that mayor, J.J.?"

"Nope. We don't want them getting the idea we're anxious. We're holding the top cards in this game and we'll keep right on playing them close to the vest. Next move's up to them."

"Yeah, seems it ought to be," Kirk agreed and rubbed nervously at his jaw. "But I keep getting the feeling they ain't about to let us ride out of here after killing that sheriff—"

"They ain't got no choice, not with us taking—"

A scream cut suddenly into Levitt's words. He sprang erect, wheeled, Deke Harvey and Kirk beside him. In the corner Rufe had seized the tall blond girl by the wrist was endeavoring to pull her out of her chair.

"Come on, sister—you and me are going over to the other room," Rufe said, laughing.

Two of the remaining girls and the teacher had come to their feet and were flailing away at Pearce with small, doubled fists.

"Let her go!" Olive Bain shouted, raking Pearce across the face with her nails.

Deke and Levitt rushed forward as Rufe struck out with his open hand. The blow caught the teacher on the side of the head, knocking her back into the chairs.

The Proving Gun

"Come on, dammit!" he snarled, jerking the blonde savagely toward him.

Deke threw himself upon the older outlaw, staggering back as Rufe slapped him hard across the face and wheeled to meet Levitt.

"Keep out of this!" he warned.

For answer J.J. lashed out with his pistol, clubbing the man solidly on the ear. Rufe cursed, dropped back a step and reached for his gun. Levitt, mouth a thin, straight line, struck again with more force.

Rufe's knees buckled but his arm continued to move. His hand came up, pistol clutched tightly. Once more J.J. rapped his outlaw partner sharply across the ear. Pearce groaned, fell heavily, his weapon clattering noisily to the floor.

Calmly holstering his pistol Levitt stepped up to the prone Rufe, and grasping him by the collar of his shirt, dragged him back to his place near the door. Then picking up Pearce's fallen weapon, J.J. thrust it under his own belt, and turned to the teacher and the girls.

Harvey had helped Olive Bain to her feet and was righting the overturned chairs. The blonde, sobbing wildly, and her companions, who had crowded, white-faced against the wall, were beginning to resume their seats.

"He won't bother you no more," Levitt said, jerking a thumb at Pearce.

"Thank you," the teacher murmured, and still holding a hand to the side of her head where Rufe's blow had fallen, turned to the sobbing girl and began to soothe her.

Nearby Deke was talking with the little dark one they called Amy. They seemed to have taken quite a shine to each other. J.J. came back around, facing Al Kirk. The gunman was studying Pearce thoughtfully.

"Reckon you know you got yourself a big problem when Rufe wakes up," he said quietly.

Levitt's mouth pulled into a hard grin. "Had myself a problem with him ever since I let him join up with us."

"He ain't going to take kindly to your batting him over the head—"

"Reckon he won't, but I ain't worrying none about it. Should've done it two, three days ago, settled him down." J.J. patted the outlaw's pistol safely tucked under his belt. "He ain't going to be so fierce now that I've drawed his fangs."

Levitt pivoted and moved toward one of the small windows that overlooked the yard and the long stretch of ground separating the schoolhouse from the town.

"Somebody ought to be showing up," he said, and then added: "but way I see it the longer they wait, the better for us. Getting away in the dark'll be just that much easier."

"If we get away at all," Kirk muttered.

Levitt stirred angrily. "Goddammit, Al, cut out your fretting!" he said impatiently, and nodded toward Olive Bain. "Right there's our ticket to Mexico, and ain't nobody going to get in our way. All we've got to worry about is how much money we'll be jingling in our pockets."

12

Tom Sutton glanced through the open doorway of his office to the crowd milling about in front of the Western Star Saloon. He'd noted its beginning earlier. It had begun to gather not long after the meeting at the bank had broken up. At first there had been only a half a dozen men— the Avery brothers, Jeremiah Teague, Jess Fallon and a couple of others. It had grown now into well over a dozen members.

The fathers of the girls being held came up well short of the ransom demanded by the outlaws, Doc Kenneman had told Sutton when he dropped by following the brief session in Henry Maxwell's place of business. Less than half the required amount of cash was available and four of the men involved—Maxwell, Jergenson, Starr and Vic Henshaw—had immediately ridden out to pay calls upon friends in the near area to ask their help in the way of loans. Teague, for reasons he kept to himself, declined to follow that procedure, remaining instead in town. A proud, unbending sort of man he had few if any acquaintances to whom he might turn and had apparently recognized the futility of making any effort.

Of course it was entirely possible Jeremiah Teague had come up with his share of the money and was now just standing by waiting for the others, Tom realized as he stepped down into the dusty street and turned toward the saloon. The tight-fisted homesteader was known to put little trust in the outside world. He could very well have had sufficient cash, and more, salted away in the slanted roof, stone and log house he'd built south of the town, and therefore found it unnecessary to seek assistance.

The rumble of conversation dwindled as Sutton approached, and by the time he had reached the crowd all talk had ceased completely. Aware of that fact, and having his wonder as to what was being said, he halted, speaking first to Teague.

"Sorry about your daughter—"

"So'm I," the homesteader said gruffly—a tall, sharp-faced individual. "It was a fool thing for her to be doing, anyway."

Tom shrugged and glanced about the silent crowd. "Olive Bain's been holding a class there every week for quite a spell. You could've—"

"Sure, I could've stopped Lucy from going, but I didn't figure there was a need. . . . Hell of a note when a man's family ain't safe in his own town."

"Place grows, attracts the wrong kind of people. Luke Jones realized that and had it in mind to warn Olive about it."

Teague looked off in the direction of the schoolhouse, not visible because of the row of business buildings.

"Too bad Luke ain't around to take care of this," he said.

Sutton's jaw tightened but he stemmed the quick spurt of temper. "I'm wishing the same thing, but I don't know what he could do that I haven't already done. My hands are tied until you and the others decide what you're going to do."

"Do!" Teague echoed bitterly. "Ain't nothing we can do

but pay up! I'm waiting on Henry Maxwell now. He's out trying to raise cash so's he can let me slap a mortgage on my place and—"

"You ain't going to get no ten thousand dollars," Jess Fallon said. "Fact is, he's working to raise enough to take care of hisself and maybe a couple of his friends."

Teague brushed nervously at his angular jaw. "Then how am I—"

"I say we ought to take things in our own hands," Pete Avery declared, moving to the top step leading onto the saloon's porch. "Them outlaws savvy only one thing and that's guns. Best thing we can do is have every man in town arm himself and then all go and throw a circle around the schoolhouse—let them know straight out they're the same as dead if they don't give in."

"What about the girls?" someone asked. "What do you think'll happen to them if we try a stunt like that?"

"Nothing worse than's probably already happened to them—or is happening right now," Avery replied.

Sutton moved in nearer to where Pete and his brother Gabe and Buffalo Finch were standing. "There'll be no more of that kind of talk," he said coldly.

Pete Avery looked down at the men facing him. "It's the truth, ain't it—and we all best admit it. If Luke was here I expect that's what he'd be planning to do."

"I doubt that," Tom said. "Luke would be thinking about those girls and the danger they'd be in if we tried storming the place."

Avery folded his arms across his chest and considered Sutton critically. "Just what are you planning, Deputy? You've got a killing and a kidnaping on your hands. You aim to just stand by and let that bunch get away with both?"

"I'm waiting until Teague here, and the others wind up their end of it. It's their daughters that are—"

"Meaning you're standing by and letting them shell out their hard-earned cash to them outlaws—and that'll be the end of it?"

"I'm keeping out of the way until those girls and Olive Bain are safe," Tom said evenly. "Then it'll be time for the law to take a hand."

"That'll be too late," Pete said caustically. "That bunch'll be long gone and you can lay odds they'll take a couple of them gals with them so's nobody'll try stopping them. Way you're figuring them outlaws'll come out smelling like a rose! They'll have the money, and will have had themselves a time with them little gals—and be getting away with murdering Luke Jones."

A shout of agreement went up from the crowd. An uneasiness began to fill Tom Sutton. He turned, glancing at Jeremiah Teague. The homesteader appeared to be in a daze and unaware of what was shaping up. That he would countenance such a foolhardy and dangerous move was unbelievable—even if the situation was desperate so far as he was concerned.

"Hell, Pete," a voice in the crowd shouted, "there's enough of us packing iron right here to handle that bunch! Only four of them, the deputy said. Let's get up there and roust them out! Luke Jones was a friend of mine and I'm for taking them out and stringing them up to the first tree we come across!"

"Forget that!" Sutton shouted, shouldering his way up onto the porch. "Nobody's going over there until we hear from Henry Maxwell and the others. It's their kin—"

"We'll be doing them a favor," Pete Avery declared.

"Anybody's a dang fool anyway if he figures them girls'll get out of there alive."

Tom threw a glance along the street. There was no sign of the banker and the other men whose daughters were captives of the outlaws. Evidently they were still out of the town attempting to raise money. He looked again at Teague. The homesteader's features had become angry.

"Pete's right," a voice said. "Let's get up there and get this thing straightened out—show that bunch they can't get away with what they're doing."

"Yeh, straighten them out by hanging them from a tree limb," another voice added with a laugh.

"No!" Tom shouted above the sudden hubbub of excitement. The mob fever was rising and could reach its peak quickly. "You don't have the right to take this into your own hands. The lives of those girls are at stake, and it's their families that have the say-so. Far as Luke Jones's murder is concerned, I'll see to that when—"

"Yeh, just like the way you let them renegades haul them girls off in the first place without trying to do something about it!"

Pete Avery raised both hands over his head to call for attention. "Teague's kid's one of them in there. Let him decide what we ought to do."

"Sure, let him do some talking—"

"What do you say, Jeremiah? You for going up to the schoolhouse, making that bunch give in?"

The homesteader again scrubbed his jaw agitatedly, and then nodded finally. "Can't see as we got much choice. I—I sure can't raise the money."

"Best you wait for the others, Teague," Sutton protested. "Those outlaws'll probably settle for a lot less than they asked for. Only thing that'll come of your trying this will be to get your daughter and some of the other girls hurt."

"Hell, they ain't about to touch them—not when they see a dozen of us waiting outside to blow their damned heads off!" Pete Avery said.

"Not the way they'll look at it—"

"What makes you think you know how to deal with a bunch of hardcases like that?" Jed Huffman demanded. The feed-store man had not committed himself one way or another up to this moment. Now he appeared to have swung over to Pete Avery's way of thinking. "Only toughs you've ever had any dealings with have been chicken thieves and drunks."

"Common sense will tell you that this sure's not the way to go about it," Sutton replied coldly, dropping a hand on the butt of his pistol. "Use your heads a little—all of you. That schoolhouse is like a fort. They can hold you off for a month if they're of a mind to."

"They won't try that when they see us all around the place and armed to the teeth. They'll mighty quick decide they ain't got a chance," Pete Avery said, and stepped down from the saloon's porch.

"Men like them live on taking chances," Sutton continued, his voice reflecting the strain that gripped him. "They won't give up like you're figuring. They all know they're living on borrowed time and—"

"Listen to the big chicken-thief-catching lawman!" someone shouted. "Knows all about hardcases and what they'll do."

As more laughter erupted Tom again swept the street with his glance hopeful of seeing Maxwell or some of the other men who were involved. There were a number of persons in sight now along the sidewalks, attracted no doubt by the noisy crowd, but there was no sign of the banker or of Ben Starr, Vic Henshaw or the storekeeper, Jergenson.

"Let's get going! We sure oughtn't to wait around till dark—"

Pete Avery, at the fringe of the gathering, again raised his hands above his head.

"Hold up a minute! We want to know for certain we're doing the right thing," he said, and turned to Teague. "We're leaving it up to you, Mr. Teague, since one of them kids inside the schoolhouse is yours. You for going up and making that bunch turn them all loose?"

The homesteader bobbed resolutely. "Don't see no other way—"

"Move out then, everybody!" Avery yelled. "Couple of you grab us some ropes—and you all be damned sure you got a'plenty of bullets and—"

"Wait!" Tom Sutton cut in, drawing his pistol. "Nobody's going near that schoolhouse—not until we hear from Maxwell and the others."

"The hell you say!" Pete Avery paused, turned, a sly grin on his lips. "Who's going to stop us?"

"I'm ordering all of you to back off, let the families of those girls and me handle this," Tom said.

"Teague's family. He's got his girl in there, and he's for it."

"There're four others besides him—and I'm speaking for Olive Bain."

"You ain't speaking for nobody," Pete said bluntly, and wheeled again to the crowd. "Everybody ready?"

A chorus of assent followed his question.

"Let's go then—"

"No!" Sutton shouted, and raising his gun, fired a warning shot into the air.

The crowd paused once more. Pete Avery came back around, the same mocking expression on his stubble-covered face.

"Now, Deputy, you ain't aiming to try stopping us, are you? You got one gun—we got maybe eighteen or twenty. Would be plumb foolish, was you to get the notion. You'd collect yourself maybe a half a dozen bullets and nobody'd ever know who fired them."

Avery studied Sutton for a long breath, spat, and then pivoting, he motioned the crowd to move on.

"Go ahead," he said in a loud voice. "The deputy ain't going to shoot none of us—not now."

13

J. J. Levitt glanced again at the clock on the wall and cursed silently. The minutes seemed to drag by like hours. What the devil was holding up the deal? Why hadn't the families of the girls they were holding kicked through with the ransom—or at least come to talk about it? Hell, he hadn't expected to get fifty thousand dollars; that had only been the starting figure.

Maybe folks weren't all he'd figured them to be, after all. An orphan since he could remember, he'd always thought a family was a tightly knit affair with each member looking out for the other and ready to fight to a finish anyone who posed a threat. Such was especially true where the head of the family—the father—was concerned. It was beginning to look now as if he'd been wrong all the way; the pas of these girls acted like they didn't give a good goddam what happened to their kids!

Levitt stirred wearily. Mexico and the ease and peace he was longing for appeared as remote now as it did a year ago when he'd made the decision to hang up his guns and quit. He'd been all but flat broke then, and here, today, after all those months that followed and all those tries at filling his poke with the money that was necessary to make his dream possible, he was as bad off as ever.

He was even worse off in one respect, thanks to Rufe Pearce. Those past few years he'd been able to keep the law off his trail pretty well. Following a system of holding up a stagecoach here, robbing a bank there with suitable layovers in between, and never using his forty-five for anything more than a club, he'd made of himself little more than a nuisance to lawmen.

Rufe, the damned fool, had changed all that for him. He'd lost his head back in Caprock and shot down those two bank clerks, and put a posse on their heels. Not only had the robbery failed but they all were being hunted for murder now. Then, to cap the jug, Rufe had stupidly killed the sheriff right here in the town where they were hoping to collect a fat ransom.

Even if the families of the girls paid off their chances now of reaching the Mexican border and the safety that lay beyond it, would be plenty slim. That was particularly so when you stopped to remember that the posse from Caprock was likely to be showing up most any time after sundown.

Maybe Mexico and the easy life wasn't in the cards for him; maybe he was slated to end up dog poor and all stove-in like a busted up bronc tamer in some two-bit town along the frontier—assuming he was lucky enough to dodge the posse from Caprock and get past the bunch here in Mimbres Crossing who'd be out to square up for the killing of their sheriff—

"Rufe's coming to—"

Kirk's low warning swung J.J.'s attention to where the outlaw lay near the door on the opposite side of the room. Deke Harvey, talking with the little dark girl he'd gotten real friendly with, rose at once and moved toward Pearce. The schoolteacher and her half circle of pupils also reacted, worry and fear stiffening their faces.

Arms folded across his chest J.J. watched Rufe get unsteadily to his feet, one hand clutching his hat that had fallen to the floor, the other gently rubbing the top of his head. His eyes narrowed slowly, began to fill with a sharp glint, and the line of his jaw hardened as his senses cleared and memory returned.

"Where's my iron?" he demanded suddenly, hand dropping to the holster on his hip.

Deke gave him no reply, simply stood rigid and quiet, a slender figure between the angry outlaw and the girls crowded together in their corner.

"I got it," Levitt said flatly.

Rufe fixed his glare on the older man, then started across the room. His legs were still a bit shaky but his whiskered face was taut.

"Hand it over!" he snarled, halting in front of Levitt.

J.J. shook his head. "Nope, I figure I'd best hang onto it. You ain't got good sense when it comes to wearing a gun."

"The hell—"

"You done proved it twice since we joined up—once back there in that bank at Caprock, and here when you cut down the sheriff."

"Them's my doings, Levitt. It's me that'll answer for it if the time comes—"

"Maybe, but me and Al and the boy'll get blamed just the same as you. . . . Anyway, I'm still calling the shots and I ain't going to let no trigger-happy gunslinger spoil my chances of getting rich."

"Give me my gun," Pearce insisted harshly, extending a hand.

"Nope," Levitt said calmly, "I'm holding onto it until we get out of here and line out for the border. You try taking it away from me and I'll buffalo you again like I done before. I ain't standing for no more killings."

"Won't be none unless somebody crowds me," Pearce said, relenting somewhat. He ducked his head at Olive and the girls. "Ain't likely one of them'll push me into using it."

J.J. smiled dryly. "Wouldn't take no bets on it, way you act. You go grabbing for iron without even thinking."

Rufe's shoulder stirred. "Hell, I was only trying to do my part," he said in a conciliatory tone. "That tin star was all set to open up on us and I was only wanting to keep him from messing up your plans. . . . Hell, getting all that money means as much to me as it does to you."

"Yeh, I reckon maybe it does," Levitt said, "but I best keep your iron till we pull out, like I told you."

"I feel sort of naked without it—"

Levitt only shrugged and for a long minute the only audible sound was the steady, monotonous ticking of the schoolroom clock.

"Ain't it about time we was hearing from them jaspers?" Pearce said, breaking the hush finally. Apparently he was abandoning his efforts to reclaim his pistol.

J.J. nodded. "That's for certain, but somebody'll be coming around pretty soon. I only give them to sundown."

"Could be they ain't planning to shell out, just sort of let us sweat."

"Ain't likely," Levitt said, denying his own earlier doubts, "but I got to admit I was looking for them to do something by now."

"They'll come," Deke Harvey said, leaning back against the wall. "Like you said, J.J., they ain't going to forget about these here girls. I know."

Levitt shifted his attention to the younger man. "You been doing some talking to them about it?"

"Yeh. Amy says they'll do what you told them. Just taking a little time to raise all that much money. Probably having to get out and borrow, she thinks. I'm still saying you oughtn't've asked for so much."

"I'm willing to dicker. All they got to do is send somebody around to do the talking."

"I ain't sure that's how they see it. Way you put it in that letter it sounded like there plain wasn't no if, and or buts—that you was wanting fifty thousand dollars, or else."

"The kid's right," Rufe said. "I'd a been satisfied with only half of what you're asking for. Man can last a long time on five or six thousand."

Al Kirk pivoted slowly and strolled leisurely to one of the windows and glanced out. "Ain't no sign of nobody coming yet," he reported, brushing away the sweat on his face with a forearm. "This stalling around's making me jumpy."

"Same here," Rufe said, throwing a glance at the girls now back on their chairs and listening quietly. "You reckon if we was to take one of them out on the landing in front of the door and start her to yelling it would stir them loose? Expect that yellow-haired gal'd squall mighty loud when I started pulling off her clothes."

"You won't need to do nothing like that," Levitt said, showing his displeasure at the suggestion. "I'll wait another hour, then if they haven't showed up, I'll send one of the girls in with the word that we're willing to bargain."

"That's a good idea," Kirk agreed. "I'd sure like to get out of here."

"That goes for me too," Rufe said. He smiled in friendly fashion at Levitt. "Sure would be obliged if you'd give me back my gun. It just don't feel right not having it."

"No, it's best I keep it," J.J. replied and started to turn away.

Rufe Pearce took a long step forward. Quick as a cat he

grasped the butt of the pistol thrust under Levitt's belt. Jerking the weapon clear, he drew back as J.J. spun to face him.

The weapon in Pearce's hand roared. Levitt jolted, staggered, a look of surprise flooding across his face. Again Rufe fired. J.J.'s knees buckled. Half twisting about, he crumpled, falling to the floor as the echoes of the two gunshots overriding the screams of the girls rocked about the room.

Half crouched in the layers of drifting smoke, pungent with the smell of burnt powder, Rufe Pearce studied Al Kirk and Harvey with his flat, narrowed eyes.

"If either one of you's aiming to make your move, now's the time to do it. You can do your trying alone or together, it makes no difference to me."

Deke Harvey settled back against the wall again and lowered his glance. Kirk's gaze held for a deep-breath longer and then he, too, turned away.

Pearce straightened slowly. "You're being smart—both of you," he said softly, and reaching down, he pulled Levitt's weapon from its holster. Shoving it under the waistband of his pants, he beckoned to Deke.

"Come over here, kid. Want you to drag the old man over into that back corner where he'll be out of the way. Then you get that yellow-haired gal and bring her to me."

Deke Harvey frowned. "What are you wanting her for?" he asked cautiously.

"Aim to stand her out there on the landing, like I said. I figure her yelling'll bring them counter-jumpers up here mighty goddam fast and—"

"Like hell you are!" Deke cut in angrily. "I ain't going—"

"You ain't going to do what?" Rufe Pearce said in a low, cold voice. "Best you get something straight right now,

93

kid. I'm running this outfit, and if that don't suit you then you—"

"They're coming," Al Kirk broke in from his place at the window. "Let's hear what they got to say before you do what you're aiming to."

14

Sutton watched the crowd, led by Pete Avery, move off into the passageway lying between the saloon and the saddlery run by Clell Adams. The schoolhouse stood a few hundred yards on to the east beyond a stretch of open, grass-covered ground.

He was simmering with anger and the urge to come down off the Western Star's porch, overtake Avery and knock some sense into the man's head was almost overpowering. But that would be the wrong way to handle it, he felt, just as using his gun would have been.

A lawman must stand on the strength of authority and not depend on violence. Besides, these were townspeople, folks who had hired him and whom he'd sworn to serve. It would be wrong to start something that could get one—or more—of them hurt. . . . Or would it? Should he have clamped down on Avery and the crowd, even if it meant shooting Pete and possibly others in the crowd who—

Sutton's thoughts came to a halt. Frowning, he glanced up to see McCandless approaching from the livery stable at a trot. And from across the street he noted Doc Kenneman, also aroused by the gunshot, hurrying up. A few persons were still collected along the sidewalk, as they had been earlier, but they were not moving, preferring to remain completely out of whatever was taking place.

"What was that shooting?" the stableman asked as he

pulled to a stop. He was breathing hard from the short run.

"Me," Sutton replied. "Trying to keep Pete Avery from leading a bunch to the schoolhouse. I was afraid they'd make things worse."

"That damned Pete," McCandless said, his eyes on the passageway into which the crowd had disappeared. "Got a mouth on him like a water bucket."

"What's going on?" Kenneman wondered, halting beside McCandless.

"Pete Avery," Tom answered, and made his explanation.

The physician snorted. "What's he up to?"

"Says he's going to make those outlaws throw down their guns and give in."

"Fat chance!" Kenneman said. "That shot—was that you trying to stop them?"

"Yeh, but it didn't do any good. I tried to talk them into waiting until Maxwell and the others showed up. They listened to Pete instead."

"You would have been doing the town a favor if you'd shot him and not wasted a bullet in the air," McCandless commented dryly.

Sutton shrugged, aware of the steady push of Doc Kenneman's eyes. Was the town's physician thinking he had failed in handling Avery and the crowd—that he was afraid to act decisively? It was possible, even likely, but it didn't matter. While he would like for Kenneman to keep on believing in him, Tom knew that he must do what he felt was right.

"Good chance I could have changed their minds if it hadn't been for Teague. He's with them—and all for it."

Kenneman wagged his head. "Jeremiah never has shown much good sense," he said, and added, "expect you should've taken steps to stop them anyway. Barging up there like they're doing could make things worse."

"That's what I tried to tell them, but the way it was, stopping them would have gotten some of them hurt—"

"Expect Doc's right," McCandless said. "You can't look at it like that. You're the law and you've got to go on what you figure's right or wrong—and if you stomp on somebody's corns doing it, it's just too bad."

"One reason why a man wearing a badge always has a shortage of close friends," Kenneman added crisply. "He can't stop to think who he's dealing with, only whether they're breaking the law. . . . Hadn't we better get over to that school—just in case—"

Sutton stepped off the saloon's porch, and together the three men hurried to overtake the crowd, now well on its way across the grassy field. As they gained the opposite end of the passageway and turned into the open, the muffled crack of pistol shots coming from within the schoolhouse reached them. Avery and his followers were also aware of the reports, and they visibly slowed their steps.

"Something's gone wrong in there," McCandless said, studying the structure as they quickened their pace. "Hope it's them outlaws killing off each other."

"Better hope one of those girls hasn't tried something foolish and got herself hurt," Kenneman said grimly. "That daughter of Ben Starr—Amy—has got a lot of spunk. Wouldn't surprise me to find out she's jumped one of that bunch."

Sutton made no comment. Trouble had developed within the schoolhouse and that brushed aside the problem of Pete Avery. He still felt he had pursued the right course where Pete and the crowd were concerned, but that was of no consequence now. Hurrying, McCandless and Kenneman at his side, he joined the cluster of men now gathered in front of the sturdy structure.

"You—inside!" Pete Avery yelled, drawing his pistol and firing a shot to draw attention. "We're giving you one minute to come out with your hands up!"

Tom shouldered his way through the crowd to Avery's side. Seizing the man by the arm, he jerked him half around.

"I'm telling you for the last time, Pete, back off and let me handle this."

Avery's dark eyes flared in surprise. His mouth hardened abruptly and he pulled away. "Who you think you're talking to, Deputy?"

"You," Sutton answered in an even voice. "I'm telling you for the last time to—"

The door of the schoolhouse swung open. A rough-looking man appeared, paused briefly, and then as if having second thoughts, he withdrew from sight.

"What the hell's he—" a man behind Avery began and then fell silent as the outlaw again stepped into view—this time with one of the girls. She was the tall, blond daughter of Karl Jergenson, and clutching her hair in one hand, holding a pistol in the other, he pushed the girl to the fore and took up a position behind her.

"You got the money?" he called in a raspy voice.

"No, and we ain't about—" Pete Avery started to reply, and broke off as Sutton, palm resting on the butt of his pistol, pushed him aside.

"Keep out of this," the lawman said.

Avery swore as he glanced around the crowd. No one

spoke up, and then McCandless said: "Best you listen to him, Pete. He'll use that gun on you if he has to—you was just lucky there a bit ago."

Avery muttered something but Sutton's attention was on the outlaw. "You the man that sent that note?"

"Nope. He ain't around no more. I'm the he bear of this outfit now. You can call me Rufe, Deputy."

"You can call me Sheriff," Tom responded coolly. "I'm giving you warning—if any of those girls get hurt it'll go hard on you."

"Sure, sure. What about the money?"

"Men are out now trying to raise it. Fifty thousand dollars is a lot of cash."

"They can get it if they're of a mind—and they sure better."

"Expect they'll come up with all they can. Meantime you go easy in there with those girls. If any of them gets hurt—"

Rufe laughed. "Ain't none of them been hurt yet," he said, and gave Katie Jergenson's hair a jerk that brought a cry of pain from her.

Anger flashed through Sutton and a muttering slipped through the crowd. A man over to Tom's left swore deeply and said, "I can pick that sonofabitch off from here easy—"

"Forget it," Sutton warned hurriedly. "There's more just like him inside."

"Somebody sure better be showing up with that money pretty soon," Rufe said, "else I ain't guaranteeing nothing."

"You gave us until dark. That's still a couple of hours off—"

"Levitt give you till dark," Rufe corrected pointedly. "Maybe I'll change my mind."

Tom shook his head. "That won't hurry things up any. There's no way we can get word to the men out raising the money. . . . What was that shooting we heard?"

The outlaw grinned. "Little personal business."

"Levitt?" Sutton pressed. He had a strong hunch they were now dealing with only three outlaws.

Rufe laughed again. "Don't fret none about him. He ain't around no more. You're doing your dealing with me, and if you've got any notions of trying to blast me and the boys out of here—"

"That's not what we're thinking—"

"I thought I heard somebody yelling for us to give up."

"It makes no difference what you thought you heard. I'm the man that's looking after things out here."

Pete Avery stirred and turned to the crowd. "This here kowtowing to them jaspers—gives me the belly-grabs! Close as we are we could rush them—"

"And get that girl killed and maybe two or three of the others," Sutton snapped. "Stay out of this, Pete."

"Teague's kid's in there and I expect he's willing to take the chance."

"Teague's not the only man concerned," Doc Kenneman replied before Tom could answer. "The sheriff told you to keep out of it, Pete. That's good advice. Follow it."

"When'll you have the money?" Rufe called. "I'm getting mighty tired of waiting."

"I already told you, it takes time," the lawman said. "But we'll have it—leastwise all they can get together. Just want to be sure you know that—and I'm warning you not to hurt any of those girls or their teacher."

"That ain't what it sounded like a bit ago. Was something about us coming out with our hands up—quitting.

The Proving Gun

Mister, if it was you saying that, you're shying rocks at the wrong dog. We don't have to give up. We're holding all the aces."

"Maybe not all of them," Sutton said, "but we're doing it your way."

"You sure better," Rufe shouted, and again yanked the Jergenson girl's hair, bringing another cry of pain from her, and a fresh wave of mumbling from the crowd.

"I'm still for rushing them," Avery said in a low voice. "Who's with me?"

"Nobody's doing anything," Sutton said flatly. "We've got to play it safe until they turn the girls loose."

Avery wagged his head and swore. "It'll be too late then. They'll be long gone."

"That'll be my problem—and I'll handle it."

"You'll handle it? What the hell you figure you can do then, Deputy?"

Tom Sutton was silent for a long moment. Then, "I'll do whatever's necessary," he said quietly and turned to the crowd. "I want you all to go home. No need for you to be here. I can't take the chance on somebody—"

"What about it, Mister Lawman?" Rufe called impatiently from the landing fronting the school's entrance. "You going to bring the money for sure or are you cooking up some kind of trick?"

"We'll have the money," Sutton answered. "Just set tight and see that nothing happens to any of those girls."

"Fair enough—but I'm changing things a mite. I ain't waiting for sundown. You got one hour to be back here with the cash."

One hour. . . . He would have to send out riders, locate Maxwell and the others and advise them of the new deadline, and hope they could make it. Sutton drew a long breath.

"All right," he said, pivoting, and with the crowd ahead of him, starting back for town. "I'll be here."

15

Olive Bain, equally shocked and stunned by the cold-blooded killing of J. J. Levitt, stood protectively in front of the girls and struggled to keep her inner feelings from them. Frightened as they were, she was their one bulwark against hysteria, and Olive knew that if she betrayed the slightest indication of breaking under the ordeal they were all experiencing, they would go to pieces with results she could not even imagine.

All, perhaps, except Amy Starr. Amy had found mutual ground with the youngest of the outlaws, Deke Harvey. Olive had endeavored to discourage their growing friendship at first but quickly discovered that her efforts were of no use; they continued to exchange sly glances and then finally to draw off to one side where they held low conversations. Eventually she gave it up and left them to their own devices, concluding that there could be some advantage to making a friend of one of the outlaws.

Now, with all of the girls except Katie Jergenson close by, she listened to the exchange of words taking place between Rufe Pearce and Tom Sutton. It was a relief to have the door open. The room was stuffy and the odor of gunpowder and smoke still filled it, but now it was gradually shifting away.

Olive glanced to the rear entrance to the school as a thought came into her mind. Deke and the older man, Al

103

Kirk, after dragging the body of J. J. Levitt into a far corner, were standing just inside the front door listening to Rufe. There was a chance—a slim one—that she and the girls could escape out the back, if they moved quickly and quietly, while the outlaws were otherwise occupied.

She gave the idea consideration, viewing it from all angles—and dismissing it. Effecting the escape without drawing the outlaws' attention would be impossible, and it would mean deserting Katie—leaving her to the mercies of Rufe Pearce—and that she could not do. Again Olive turned her attention to the exchange underway in front of the school.

She had not recognized the voice of the first speaker, the one who had yelled for the outlaws to surrender, but Tom Sutton had taken over and was now speaking for the people gathered outside. He appeared to be very much in command of the situation and while he didn't know just when the ransom would be paid, it did look as if he was able to reassure Pearce and calm him down somewhat.

Rufe, upon hearing the first voice and the demand that they surrender, had gone into a rage. He'd cursed wildly, declaring if the townspeople wanted a shootout, he'd be more than happy to oblige them, and with a pistol in each hand, had started for the door.

Abruptly he'd changed his mind, and turning back, had come to where she and the girls were standing. Seizing Katie Jergenson by the arm, and despite her attempts to stop him, he had dragged Katie out onto the landing with him.

Deke and Al Kirk had looked upon Rufe's actions with a sort of scorning disfavor, but they'd made no move to interfere. They were afraid to oppose Rufe, there was no doubt of that, and Olive guessed she couldn't blame them.

After the merciless way he'd shot down his friend and partner, Levitt, they had every right to think twice before defying him.

You gave us until dark, she heard Tom say. *Still a couple of hours off.*

He'd taken over Luke Jones's job and was handling it well, Olive thought. Unquestionably the sheriff was dead, or dying, and Tom Sutton would assume the position of town lawman officially. She was happy to know he would be getting what he wanted but it was too bad that a man had to be killed to bring it about.

Tom had looked forward to the time when he would become sheriff and had talked with her about that and his future several times. She guessed she'd been a little short with him on most occasions and had studiously discouraged his hints and intimations that they could have a life together for she really hadn't been interested.

Now she discovered she was looking at things in a different light; the Tom Sutton she was hearing speak, who was yielding not at all to Rufe Pearce while still skillfully keeping the situation under control, was not the man she'd known before.

Here was a new, strong Tom Sutton, one in which a great change had taken place. He no longer sounded unsure of himself, hesitant and deferential with others as he formerly had been. The death of Luke Jones could be thanked for that, too, Olive thought again ruefully. Tom had suddenly been pushed out on his own, was being forced to stand on his own feet, and without the advice and aid of the older lawman, make his own decisions.

It was unfortunate that he had to come up against outlaws like Rufe Pearce and the men he had running with him right at first. It would have been easier on him if he had been able to face up gradually to the worst sort of lawlessness. Still, maybe it was all for the best. Tom Sutton would emerge from this confrontation either a proven lawman or a total failure, and if it developed the latter was true he would do well to find a different way of life and do so while he was young.

What about it, Mister Lawman? Olive heard the taunting voice of Rufe Pearce call. *You going to bring the cash for sure or are you cooking up some kind of a trick?*

And then came Tom's confident, reassuring answer. *We'll have the money. Just set tight and see that nothing happens to any of those girls.*

Olive glanced at Dulcie Henshaw, then huddled against her and at the other girls close by. Their faces were chalk white, and except for Amy Starr, their eyes were red from weeping. She smiled.

"Tom will see to it that everything comes out all right. Don't worry."

Her own words of confidence surprised her somewhat, but they sounded good in her own ears, and she knew at once that she meant them. There had been a change in her feelings toward Tom Sutton and it was not due entirely to the fact that in all likelihood he would be the one who would stand between her and the girls, and the outlaws when the final moments came.

The door kicked back and Pearce, now holding on to Katie Jergenson by an arm, re-entered the room. The talk was over and Tom, along with whoever else was with him, would be making the walk back to town. Olive hoped it would not take much longer for him to get the money and return; she was not sure she could maintain her control for many more minutes.

She drew up slowly, eyes on Pearce and Katie. The outlaw had not released his grip on the girl and was looking off into the adjoining room. Rufe's face had the shine of sweat on it and his lips were pulled into a taut grin.

Fear rose abruptly within Olive Bain, and then gathering her courage, she moved out of the corner where she and the others stood, and crossing the room, took the seemingly dazed Jergenson girl by the hand.

"Come on, Katie," she said firmly, and pulled her away from the outlaw.

The grin faded from Rufe's lips and a scowl crossed his face. He started to say something, and then perhaps recalling Tom Sutton's words, he released his hold on the tall blonde, shrugged, and turning to the still open door, kicked it shut.

"I give them one hour to show up with the cash," he said, bucking his head at Kirk and Deke Harvey. "One hour—that's all they're getting."

"What if they don't make it?" Deke asked.

Olive, leading Katie into the corner paused to hear Pearce's answer.

"Then we stall around till dark and head for the border," Rufe said. "And we won't be going alone."

Tom, turning about, allowed the crowd to move off ahead of him. McCandless, hanging back briefly, stepped up beside him and nodded approvingly.

"You done real fine, Sheriff—just what you ought've," the stable owner said. "That Pete Avery'd got somebody killed sure'n hell if he'd had his way."

Tom shrugged. "Obliged, but there wasn't much I could do except try to keep that bunch leveled off until Maxwell and the others show up. We've got to get word to them somehow, let them know the deadline's been changed."

"Reckon they're still out making calls on their friends, trying to borrow money. I heard Maxwell say he had less'n ten thousand in the bank they could use. This time of year everybody's short."

Sutton looked ahead. Pete Avery, with his brother Gabe and friend Buffalo Finch, had dropped back, allowing the crowd to continue. On beyond them Doc Kenneman, his steps hurried, was entering the passageway between the saloon and the Gun & Saddle Shop, apparently answering a call from his office.

Somewhere off in the direction of Mimbres Creek a gunshot flatted through the warm stillness and the far-off barking of a dog was a faint, lonely sound.

"You figuring what you'll do after you hand the money over to that bunch?" McCandless asked.

"Not for sure. I'll have to see how it goes. Main thing is to get Olive and those girls in the clear, then decide."

"It's going to be awful hard on the town if they get away with that money. Could about break it."

"I know that, but it'll be worse if anything happens to the girls. They come first, the way I see it."

"Sure," McCandless hastened to say. "I didn't mean for you to think they shouldn't—I'm just trying to figure how this maybe'll turn out. You going to have a posse waiting somewheres between here and the border ready to crack down on them when they show up?"

"I'll have to decide that later. Be my guess they'll take one of the girls along as a hostage to guarantee a safe passage to Mexico. If so, a posse's out of the question. I'll have to go it alone. Be the only safe thing I can do. If they don't, then we'll have a dozen men ready—"

Tom slowed his steps, coming to a halt. They had

reached the area behind the saloon. Pete Avery, sided by Gabe and Finch, were blocking his way.

Bristling, McCandless moved a stride ahead of the young lawman. "What's this?" he demanded.

"Ain't none of your butt-in, so keep out of it, old man," Pete said. "Me and the deputy's got a little settling to do."

McCandless swore. "What the hell's eating you, Pete? Man's only trying to do his job."

"He's got something else to do right now unless he's a mite short on guts," Avery said.

The stableman swore again. "He ain't got time to fool with you—and you damn well know it. He needs to send word to—"

"Reckon somebody else can do that," Pete broke in. "I'm going to teach him it ain't healthy to go shoving folks like me around."

"You're loco, Pete," McCandless said in disgust. "Why'n't you move on—"

Sutton laid a hand on the older man's shoulder and drew him back. "Never mind," he said quietly. "It's my problem."

Avery, legs spread, big fists hanging at his sides, smiled mockingly. "How about it, Deputy? You fighting or running?"

"Fighting," Tom replied in a clipped voice, and taking a long step forward drove a hard right into Avery's jaw.

Surprised, Pete staggered back. The grin vanished from his lips, and ducking low, he charged, both arms pumping like pistons. Sutton took several blows to the middle, pivoted to one side, paused and sent a down-sledging left to Avery's ear.

Pete grunted, dropped to both knees. He came up quickly, again charged. Tom once more spun away, and as

The Proving Gun

he came back around, straightened Avery with an upper-cut, following that with a straight left that caught Pete flush on the chin.

Avery swore, retreated a few steps. Halting, mouth hanging open as he sucked for breath, head slung forward, he considered Sutton narrowly. That he had expected to have an easy time with Tom was evident. Now, aware of his error, he decided to take the matter more seriously.

Lowering his head, in a complete change of tactics, Pete moved in slowly. His knotted fists were up, and abandoning his previous reckless charging, he advanced cautiously seeking an opening. Sutton backed away, began to circle warily, his own guard set. Off to the side Gabe Avery and Finch were now talking continuously, urging Pete on, offering advice and encouragement but doing so under the watchful eyes of Bill McCandless who, having scooped up Sutton's pistol when it dropped from its holster, was holding it in his hand.

Abruptly Pete Avery lashed out with his left, missed, swung a hard right. Sutton took the blow high on a shoulder, spat to rid himself of the dust stirred up by their scuffing boots that had collected in his mouth, and countered with a short jab that rocked Avery's head. Before he could pull aside Pete nailed him with a shocking blow to the ribs that exploded breath from his lungs, followed with another to the belly. Staggering, Tom sought to wheel away. Instantly Pete kicked out, knocking Sutton's feet from under him.

Suddenly flat on the ground, Sutton rolled quickly but he was too slow to avoid a second kick that caught him in the small of the back. With the outraged cursing of McCandless and the shouts of glee from Gabe and Buffalo Finch in his ears, Tom continued to roll, then bounded

110

upright. Anger surging through him, he spun, ducked low as Pete, hungry for the kill, closed in.

Locking both hands together into a double fist, Sutton stopped short, straightened, and swung a wide, round-house blow. It connected with the side of Avery's head with such force that it sent the man sprawling into the dust. Stunned, he started to rise. Raging, Sutton moved in on him, drove him back with a right to the jaw.

Reaching down, Tom grasped the prostrate man by the shirt front, dragged him upright, and supporting the sagging Avery with one hand, he smashed another blow to his chin with the other. Pete Avery's head snapped back and lolled to the side. Sutton drew back his arm to deliver another punishing blow, then hesitated. For a long moment he stared at the limp figure sagging in his grasp, and then released his hold, allowing Avery to fall.

"Sheriff—"

Heaving for wind, Sutton turned to the speaker. In the heat of the battle he had not been conscious of others coming in from the street and gathering alongside McCandless to watch. Now, flicking the small crowd with a glance, he turned to the speaker.

"Yeh?" he answered, taking his gun from the livery stable owner.

"They want you at the bank." It was Artie Jenkins, one of Henry Maxwell's clerks. "They've got the money together—what they could raise—and they're ready for you to take it to the schoolhouse."

16

Tom nodded, brushed the dust from his pistol and slid it into its holster. He turned slowly, laid his still burning eyes on Pete Avery, now, with the aid of his brother and Buffalo Finch, pulling himself to his feet.

"This end it?" Sutton asked in a tight voice.

Avery, dust plastered, a streak of blood at one corner of his mouth and the left side of his face discoloring rapidly, stared woodenly at the lawman.

"No, it don't," Gabe Avery said, taking it upon himself to answer for his brother. "He'll be looking to—"

"It does far as I'm concerned," Sutton broke in sharply. "I'm ordering the three of you to move on. I don't want to see any of you in Mimbres Crossing after dark tomorrow. And if I ever find you in my town again after that I'll—"

"Hell—you can't run us off!" Gabe declared angrily.

"I can—and I am," Sutton stated flatly, and turning on a heel, headed for the street.

McCandless, hurrying to keep pace with the lawman, and followed by Jenkins and the half a dozen or so passers-by who had witnessed the altercation, muttered under his breath. Tom glanced about at the stable owner.

"Something bothering you?" he asked. His voice was still taut.

McCandless wagged his head. "Ain't so sure you done the right thing back there."

"You think I ought've let Pete walk all over me?"

"No, don't mean that. He asked for a licking and he sure'n hell got one. I'm thinking it'd maybe been better if you'd a left it right there."

"Not run him and his brother and that friend of theirs off—that what you're driving at? They're nothing but saloon bums, drunks—thieves. Town will be better off without them laying around."

"Ain't saying it won't, only it'd been better if you'd a'let Pete and the others make up their own minds that this weren't no place for them, that you plain didn't want them hanging about. Going to look to some like you was showing off your authority by—"

"Oh, the hell with it!" Sutton muttered in sudden disgust, and entering the street, angled toward the bank.

It seemed to Tom Sutton that he was having a difficult time doing anything right; he was criticized if he did, criticized if he did not. As Luke Jones had said, no matter which course he took in settling a situation, he was going to bring down the wrath of someone upon his head. . . . And Luke had said something else—something that he had forgotten.

"You'll be wearing the star, and that stands for authority. You don't have to prove what that badge means, only that you're big enough to wear it—not strong enough, mind you, but big enough."

Tom reckoned that was what Bill McCandless was trying to say. There was no need to order Pete Avery and the two others out of town; the fact that Pete had started something that he couldn't finish, and had been thoroughly humbled before those he sought to impress, was probably all that was necessary to rid Mimbres Crossing of his presence. The law had taken no nonsense from him and put him in his place. Nothing else on its part was needed.

Tom slowed as he approached the bank. A cluster of a dozen or more persons were collected around the doorway, and making his way through them, with McCandless at his heels, he entered the small, darkened building. Henry Maxwell, with ranchers Vic Henshaw and Ben Starr, store owner Karl Jergenson, and the homesteader Jeremiah Teague, who earlier had stood by Pete Avery and his scheme to flush out the outlaws in the schoolhouse, were awaiting him in the banker's private office.

"Where the hell you been?" Jergenson demanded irritably.

"He was at the school keeping Pete Avery and some others from getting them girls of your'n hurt," Bill McCandless snapped. "Teague, there, could've told you that if you'd asked him."

Jergenson frowned and scrubbed at his jaw nervously. Strain was showing on his features, just as it was on the four other men whose daughters were involved. Elsewhere in the building several women were waiting, some rigid and silent, others weeping raggedly.

"We couldn't raise the fifty thousand," Maxwell said. "Explain to those men, tell them we tried, that we borrowed from everybody we could, but folks are short of cash this time of year. You have to make them understand that, Sheriff."

"I'll do all I can," Sutton assured the banker. "How much did you come up with?"

"Less than half the amount—around twenty-one thousand."

"Somebody said there was shooting up there," Ben Starr

114

said grimly. "If they've hurt any one of those girls you can tell them for me that they'll pay, by God, if it takes—"

"I don't think it had anything to do with your daughters," Tom said. "Looks to me like there's been a falling out between them. Man that's running things now calls himself Rufe. Name on the note Olive Bain wrote was Levitt, and Rufe made it plain that Levitt was out. Whether that means he's dead or not, I don't know."

"You figure you can handle this all right?" Henshaw asked.

Tom Sutton smiled faintly. "There's no choice. Orders from them were that I was to bring it. Means they aim to get me out of the way so's they can ride on without any trouble."

"Maybe that's what they're figuring, but that sure ain't how it's going to be," Ben Starr said hotly.

Sutton raised a hand quickly. "Best you forget that," he warned. "You can bet they'll be taking one or maybe a couple of the girls along as hostages so's we won't try to stop them. We try heading them off with a posse whoever they've taken with them is sure to get hurt. . . . I want you to leave it all up to me."

"I don't know about that," Henshaw said slowly. "We sure can't afford to let them reach the border with all that money."

"That's not what I'm planning either, but they're calling the shots, at least for now. After I get inside and find out what they're planning, then I'll know what we can do. Meantime you're to sit tight—all of you—wait for word from me."

"Wait," Henshaw echoed protestingly.

"That's what I said, and I want it made clear to everybody."

"You aiming to do it all—deliver the money, set the girls free and catch them renegades all by yourself, Deputy, that it?" Jergenson said in a scornful tone. "That's a pretty tall order."

Tom shrugged. "I never asked them to pick me to deliver the money. Anyway, that's how it'll have to be until they make their move. If they just grab the money and ride out, leaving the girls be, all well and good. We'll need a posse then. But if they do like I think they will and hang onto some hostages, that's something else."

"That mean we just let them off scot free?" Maxwell wondered.

"No, it'll be up to me to go after them. One rider alone won't be noticed by them, and I should be able to catch up fast. Then I can watch my chances, move in. It'll be dark so it ought to be fairly easy to free the hostages and recover your money—all depending of course on whether they're going to settle for less than half the ransom they wanted in the first place."

"Best we could do," Henry Maxwell said wearily. "I'd be willing to fork over the whole amount if I had it. My daughter means that much to me."

"Same here," Ben Starr said, "but goddammit, they didn't give us no time. You got to make them see that, Sheriff, if they put up a holler."

"I'll do my best," Tom said, and turned to Bill McCandless. "I'd like for you to have my horse ready and standing in that shed behind the jail. Don't let them see you putting him there."

"Sure, Tom—what about a posse?"

"Round up a dozen or so men, get them mounted. Best you keep them out of sight too—keeping them waiting in your stable will be a good idea."

"But how'll we know if they're to take out after that bunch?" Henshaw asked, frowning.

"I'll give you a signal," Sutton explained. "Keep your eyes on that window in the south wall of the schoolhouse. Like as not they'll tie up the girls and me before they leave, but I'll manage to give you a sign of some kind. If you see something it'll mean they've taken the money and rode off without hostages—and you're to go after them."

"And if we don't see no signal?"

"Then you sit tight—do nothing. It'll all be up to me. I'd like to borrow a knife from somebody—"

McCandless drew a bone-handled skinning blade from the scabbard hanging from his belt. "This do?"

Sutton nodded, and bending down, slipped the knife into his left boot. Vic Henshaw stirred restlessly.

"What'd be wrong with just a couple of us waiting down the line a way—even if they do take one of the girls with them?"

"Too big a risk far as I'm concerned," Sutton replied, "but it's up to you. If you want to gamble on being able to stop them without getting the hostages hurt, I'll forget my plan."

"We'll do it your way," Henry Maxwell said quickly. "We won't make a move unless we see a signal of some kind in that window."

"That's it. If you do it'll mean the girls are safe and you can do whatever you want."

"I'm hoping that's how it'll be," Henshaw said, grinding out his words. "Nothing'll suit me better than to get a couple of them renegades in my rifle sights."

"That goes for all of us I reckon, Vic," Starr added quietly.

"It would be the easy way for all of us, but I doubt

you'll get the chance," Tom said, picking up the saddle-bags containing the money and hanging them across a shoulder. "They're too smart to leave themselves wide open like that."

Maxwell took a step forward and extended his hand. "I don't know whether you realize the chance you're taking or not, Sheriff. Once you're inside that schoolhouse anything can happen. I want you to know that I, for one, am grateful to you."

"That goes for all of us," Starr said, glancing about. "Maybe we haven't shown it but we mean it just the same. Only that we've all been mighty worried and stirred up—"

Sutton smiled. "That's not hard to understand."

Jeremiah Teague, ruddy face dark, mouth set to a tight line, nodded slowly. "Reckon I'm the one that needs to do some apologizing, Sheriff. That was a fool thing I done. I don't know what got into me."

"It's all over and done with now," Tom said. "Best we forget it."

"You take my hand on that?" the homesteader continued.

"Sure," Sutton replied, and took the tall man's fingers into his own. Pressing them briefly, he turned to McCandless. "Don't forget my horse—and keep everybody away from the schoolhouse. Seeing a bunch of people standing around watching's liable to make them jumpy."

"Leave it to me, Tom," the stableman said. "Good luck."

"Expect I'll be needing it," Sutton answered with a humorless grin, and crossing to the doorway, stepped out into the street.

17

The crowd outside the bank had increased, and as Sutton appeared, it parted silently allowing him to pass through. Down in front of the Western Star he saw Pete Avery slouched against the wall of that building. Nearby were his brother Gabe and Buffalo Finch. They watched him narrowly as he headed into the passageway lying between the bank and Jergenson's store.

Tom considered the trio briefly and dismissed them from his mind; he'd given them until the next day's sundown to ride out. He'd look for them then, be certain they'd moved on—assuming he was still alive.

Breaking out into the open behind the row of structures lining the east side of the street, Sutton started across the flat for the schoolhouse. It was a strange, lonely feeling— the absolute quiet, the absence of all other persons and signs of life—and knowing for certain the outlaws inside the classrooms were watching him closely and most likely with guns drawn and leveled in the event he attempted any trickery.

Midway he paused to adjust the saddlebags. Heavy with silver and gold coin, and paper money, they were continually sliding down onto his arm. Moving on, Tom glanced at the sun; he was well within the hour limit Rufe had prescribed so there should be no problem where time was concerned.

But he could be in for deep trouble otherwise, Sutton knew. It was impossible to predict just what course the outlaws would follow. They could do as he had assumed; accept the money, and after disarming him, tie him securely and ride out taking with them one or more of the girls as a guarantee of safe passage.

He was prepared for that, just as he had formulated his plan of action should they simply seize the cash and make a run for it, relying on their horses and guns to outwit and outmaneuver any posse that followed them.

However, they could have some other altogether different scheme in mind, something he had overlooked completely. He had taken much on himself, Tom realized, when insisting the townspeople leave the matter up to him —and likely there would be many who would believe he had taken his strong, perhaps arbitrary stand simply to convince others that he was a capable lawman.

In reality this had not occurred to him. He was thinking only of the hostages and their safety which, insofar as he was concerned, took priority over the money involved. But if he failed to recover the cash, once the girls were in the clear, he could expect to come in for a great deal of criticism born of hindsight; the fact that no harm had come to the hostages would slip into the background and the calamitous loss of the money would become foremost in the memories of Mimbres Crossing's citizenry.

Maybe he should have agreed to a posse being dispatched and stationed down the valley where it could intercept the outlaws as they made their dash for the border. A dozen men certainly should be able to stop four; but the fear that harm might befall any hostage accompanying Rufe and his partners had been uppermost in his thoughts and outweighed the possibility of any personal censure that might befall him later. In his own judgment Tom Sutton felt he was right, but riding shoulder to shoulder with that conviction was the knowledge that should it turn out that he was wrong his career as a lawman would end almost before it had begun.

The schoolhouse loomed in his vision. Sutton halted, again adjusted the slipping saddlebags. It seemed to him there should have been some reaction to his approach by that moment.

"Hello—inside!" he shouted, raising his hands above his head.

The door opened. No one appeared. A long breath followed and then the outlaw who called himself Rufe, evidently first having a careful look around to be certain the lawman was alone, stepped partly into view.

"Keep coming, Deputy. And keep your hands up just like you got them."

Sutton, tension rising steadily within him, resumed his slow march. Reaching the square landing, he stepped up onto it, crossed and entered the room.

Immediately he felt the hard, round muzzle of Rufe's pistol jam into his side, then the change of weight on his hip as the outlaw lifted his own weapon from its holster. A thud followed as the gun was tossed into a near corner.

There were only three of them, Tom noted, his eyes sweeping the shadow-filled area. Evidently Levitt, in a dispute of some kind, had been killed. Olive and the girls, huddled against the opposite wall, appeared to be unhurt. When they recognized him, one, he could not tell who she was, began to sob with relief.

Rufe, a hard-visaged man with small eyes, jerked the saddlebags off Tom's shoulder, threw them to the floor and motioned to one of the other outlaws—a small, considerably older individual. The red bandanna the man was wearing stirred Sutton's memory; he was the stranger that Luke Jones had noted emerging from the Poor Man's Saloon.

"See how much is there, Al," Rufe directed.

The outlaw knelt over the bags and began to unbuckle the straps.

"Twenty-one thousand," Sutton said, placing his attention on Rufe. "That was all they could raise on such short notice."

Rufe swore vividly. "Hell a-mighty, that ain't even half—"

"That's the best they could do. They borrowed most of that from folks up and down the valley."

The third outlaw, a young, light-haired, light-eyed boy still in his teens, moved in closer and halted beside Al.

"That's aplenty," he said. "Splitting it only three ways now means seven thousand dollars apiece."

Rufe swore again and holstered his gun. "Yeh, reckon if it's the best they could do there we'll have to be happy. Let's get out of here."

"Might be smart to divvy up the cash here and now," Al said, picking up the saddlebags and rising. "We just might run into a posse and have to scatter."

"There ain't going to be no posse," Rufe stated, and taking the leather pouches from the older man, slung them over his shoulder. "I aim to take that yellow-haired gal along with us. That'll keep them counter-jumpers from trying to head us off."

At his words, a cry broke from the lips of the girl mentioned—Katie Jergenson, Tom saw. She sank back against the wall, collapsed slowly to the floor in a dead faint. At once Olive Bain bent over her.

The Proving Gun

"Best you forget that one," Al said. "Sort of sickly like
and she won't be nothing but trouble. Take one of the
others." He paused, jerking a thumb at Sutton. "What're
we doing with him?"

Rufe favored the lawman with a scowling glance. "Tie
him up, leave him laying here. Use that rawhide Levitt's
using as a belt. Get it and take care of him, Deke," he
added, turning to the younger outlaw, "bring up the
horses. We'll be needing Levitt's."

"What for?" the boy wondered.

"So's the teacher'll have something to ride, that's what
for!" Rufe shouted, exasperated. "I told you we'd be taking
us a hostage. Ain't you been listening?"

"Yeh, sure, only I was—"

"Only you got your eye so set on that little black-headed
one you can't think of nothing else."

Deke straightened up, facing Rufe squarely. "She's
coming with us."

The outlaw shook his head. "Don't need but one," he
said, watching Al return from the adjoining room where he
had obtained a length of leather cord.

"She ain't going to be no hostage. She's going to Mexico
with me."

Rufe's brows lifted and he grinned broadly. "The hell
you say! Fixing yourself up with a woman, that it? Kid,
you're growing up!"

Sutton, attention on the girls, saw Olive half rise. Shock
stilled her features. The knowledge that she was being
taken along as hostage and that one of the girls had cast
her lot with the young outlaw was having its effect upon
her. Immediately Ben Starr's daughter, Amy, moved away
from her and the remaining girls, a half smile on her lips,
and joined the boy.

"Put your hands behind you—"

At Al's command Tom changed the position of his arms, crossed his wrists and waited while the outlaw bound them together. So far he had not been searched, and the knife in his boot had gone undetected. He would have some difficulty in getting it with his hands tied together so tightly, but it could be done. There was a good chance he wouldn't need to make the effort, however; Rufe, fearing nothing from the girls he would be leaving in the room, likely would not bother to bind them, and he could enlist their aid in freeing himself.

"I told you to get the horses," Rufe said, motioning impatiently to Deke. "Sooner we light out for the border, the better I'll be liking it. . . . You figuring on your gal riding double with you? We ain't got no extra horse."

"She'll be riding with me," the younger man said, and wheeling, headed for the rear entrance to the school, Amy Starr with him.

Al, his chore finished, stepped to the window and glanced out. Sutton eyed the man nervously, fearful he might do something that could be interpreted by those watching at the edge of town as a signal. But he merely had his brief look, satisfied himself that all was well outside, wheeled and came back to where Rufe, attention on Olive Bain and the girls, was standing.

"Sure wish't it was the little yellow-haired gal that I'll be taking along," Rufe said, "but we ain't got time to be playing nursemaid to nobody—and that's what she'd be needing all the way. I'll just have to be happy with the teacher, I reckon. You all ready for some riding, Teacher?"

Tom, shoulders to the wall, studied Olive. She was standing rigidly erect, face pale, eyes partly closed, lips a firm, straight line. He nodded slightly, hoping to reassure her. Beyond her one of the girls had begun to cry.

When Olive made no reply, Rufe laughed. "Sure you're ready! I can see it plain," he said, and turned to Sutton. He pointed to the lawman's new star.

"Reckon you can thank me for that, Deputy. I got you promoted plenty quick."

Tom studied the outlaw coldly. "It was you then that shot Luke Jones—"

"If that was the name of that sheriff, it sure was. He made the wrong move—"

At that moment Deke, with Amy Starr clinging to his hand, appeared in the doorway. "Horses're ready. We're set to go."

"Good enough," Rufe said, and swung back to Sutton. "I figure you ain't damn fool enough to try something—not with me keeping two hostages—"

"Amy ain't no hostage!" Deke cut in indignantly.

"Course she ain't—I was only putting it that way," Rufe said, grinning, and returned again to the lawman. "Like I was saying, I figure you ain't no fool so I'm just leaving you here sort of tied up so's you won't get in the way while we're leaving. Now, there sure better not be no posse hanging around—"

"There's not," Tom said, controlling the anger in his voice. Besides the cold, indifferent way the outlaw was carrying out the kidnaping he had calmly admitted the murder of Luke Jones, even making a sort of joke of it. "When will you turn the girls loose?"

"You meaning the teacher? Oh, come morning, I expect —if we don't run up against some trouble. Up to the kid what he does with that'n he's got."

"I'm going to stay with Deke," Amy Starr said firmly. "We're going to get married and live in Mexico."

Olive Bain's stiff figure relented. She faced the girl. "Don't be a fool, Amy—"

"What's wrong with that?" Amy demanded defensively. "I'm tired of school, of living on a ranch and doing—"

"Time we was pulling out," Rufe broke in, moving toward the door. He made an abrupt, off-hand gesture at Al. "Grab the teacher and put her on Levitt's horse—and you best hang onto the leathers till we're started. We don't want her trying to get away."

The outlaw strolled casually across the room, displaying no haste, utterly secure in his belief that he would encounter no opposition as he and his party took their leave. And they wouldn't, Tom knew, unless someone in town foolishly ignored his instructions.

Al, flicking his partner with a brief, curling glance, stepped up to Olive, and grasping her by the arm, propelled her through the open doorway to where the horses were waiting. Beyond them Sutton could see the Starr girl swinging up behind Deke and settling herself on the back of his saddle.

Rufe paused and glanced around. "Sure much obliged to you, Sheriff. You been mighty helpful," he drawled, and then was gone from sight.

18

Immediately a sob of relief burst from the girls huddled in the corner of the room. One began to scream, giving way finally to the hysteria pent up within her. Sutton crossed to them in a half a dozen lunging strides.

"Somebody!" he shouted, striving to break through the confusion. "Help me! Get the knife out of my boot—cut me loose!"

There was no reaction. Tom, counting the fleeting moments subconsciously, crowded in close. Putting a shoulder against the nearest girl, Charity Maxwell, he jostled her roughly. She drew back, turning her tear-stained face to him.

"There's a knife in my boot—the left one," he said. "Get it!"

Charity stared at him woodenly for a long moment and then knelt, obtaining the knife. As she straightened up, Sutton wheeled, placed his back to her and extended his bound wrists.

"Cut the rope! I've got to go after them," he said then, as he felt the leather cord part. "You take care of your friends and get them back to town. Can you do it?"

Charity nodded. "The surrey—I guess it's still in the shed."

"Expect it is. Now, when you see your pa tell him that

I'm following them—and that he's to forget the posse. You understand?"

"He's to forget about the posse," Charity repeated dully.

"That's it. I made it clear to him and the others before I came here—I just want to be certain they remember. I've got to do this alone otherwise we could get Olive and Amy hurt."

"Amy—what will I tell her folks? She went with that outlaw—going to marry—"

Sutton had turned away, crossing the room to where Rufe had tossed his pistol. Retrieving it, he checked its action and slid it into the holster.

"Maybe you better not tell them about Deke. Just let them think she's a hostage, like Olive. Could be I'll get a chance to talk her out of what she's doing. Tom paused at the door, eying the girl narrowly. "You going to be all right?"

Charity nodded and managed a smile. The remaining girls, realizing the ordeal was now over, had regained their composure and were dabbing at their eyes with handkerchiefs and straightening their clothing.

"We'll be fine—"

Sutton opened the door and stepped out into the lowering sunlight. Still a couple of hours until full dark, he noted, breaking into a run. If he could get to his horse and make it to Sentinel Point, a high upthrust of rock standing at the end of the Mulehead Mountains, there would still be light enough for him to have a good look at the country down which the outlaws, with Olive and Amy Starr, would have to travel. Locating them would simplify his plan to cut across the valley and lie in wait since he would know just where to set up an ambush.

Breathing hard, Sutton reached the shed behind the jail

and veered into it. He heaved a sigh of relief; Bill McCandless hadn't forgotten. His bay gelding was standing ready to ride in the shelter. Jerking the reins free of the ring in the wall, he led the horse into the open and swung onto the saddle. Anger rolled through him as two men appeared suddenly before him—coming from the shadows alongside the jail—the Avery brothers. Pete had his gun out and leveled.

"Crawl down off that nag," Pete said through badly swollen lips. "You ain't going nowheres."

"Get out of my way," Tom replied coldly, making no move to comply.

"Not much I am. You got a beating coming to you. Ain't nobody knocks me around the way you done and gets away with it."

"If you want to try your luck again, wait until I get back. You know what's happened. Those outlaws've got Olive Bain and Ben Starr's daughter. I've got to stop them—"

"I know all about it, sure," Pete said. "We seen them— but I reckon they'll have to wait."

"No—"

"Maybe we best let him go on, Pete," Gabe said uncertainly. "Letting them gals get hurt'll sure stir up folks against us plenty, and we—"

"Ain't nothing going to happen to them because this ain't going to take long. Anyway, soon's I'm done working this jasper over, we'll light out and catch up. I got me a idea how we can fix ourselves up real good."

"You claiming you saw them go by?" Sutton asked, impatient but quietly calculating the odds for an escape.

"Sure—they was heading for the border," Gabe said.

"On the road?"

"Nope; they was following it, howsomever and—"

"Shut up, goddammit!" Pete snarled. "You ain't no newspaper! You coming off that horse, Deputy?"

Tom ignored the question. Evidently Rufe and the men with him did not know the alternate route to Mexico, and were relying on the usually traveled road while taking care not to be seen on it. He wouldn't need to make the ride to Sentinel Point; he could cut diagonally across the flats and be waiting at the bluffs, well ahead of them.

Of course there was the possibility that Amy Starr would know of the more direct trail that ran due south, and beguiled as she appeared to be by the young outlaw Deke, did not call it to his attention. He could only gamble on that. He could be certain Olive Bain would not mention it, if she knew. Sutton centered his attention again on Pete Avery.

"I'm telling you for the last time—holster that gun and get out of my way. I've got a job to do."

"We figure to do it for you, Deputy," Pete said, and reached for the bay's reins.

Tom reacted instantly. He jammed his spurs into the gelding's flanks. The big horse, startled, lunged forward, swerving to avoid Pete. He was too close. His shoulder drove into Avery, knocked him aside, and sent him sprawling onto the ground. The pistol in Pete's hand went off, the bullet harmlessly driving into the wall of the shed as Sutton, crouched low on the saddle, raced for the trees bordering Mulehead Creek.

He reached them and glanced back. There had been no second shot and he guessed Pete Avery had been stunned and unable to recover in time. Gabe, who showed a reluctance to carry on whatever his brother had in mind, had made no effort to stop him. Pete was on his feet now, he

saw, and Gabe had dropped back, bringing up their
horses. Tom gave that some thought as the bay, fording
the shallow stream, climbed its opposite bank; would they
follow?

He swore, considering the possibility. The way Pete felt
about him, it was most likely. Avery had a big urge burning inside him to even the score, and one effective means
would be to prevent him from going through with his plan
to overtake the outlaws, free the girls and recover the
money.

Sutton smiled grimly as he put the bay gelding to a gal-
lop in the gathering darkness. He had made an issue of it
with the people of Mimbres Crossing, insisting they permit
him to handle the situation. They had agreed, some with
little enthusiasm; now if he were to fail. . . .

Sutton shook off the thought, throwing a glance over his
shoulder. The shadows were lengthening between the
trees and he could see no sign of Pete and Gabe Avery,
but there was little reassurance in that. Darkness was
already limiting visibility.

He rode on, pulling the bay down to a fair lope. He
couldn't afford to worry about the Avery brothers; he must
put his mind to what lay ahead. With night closing about
him, shutting off his hoped-for view of the country, he
could only guess where Rufe and the others might be, and
hope all the while they had not changed course.

That the outlaws were striking for Mexico was, of
course, a foregone conclusion. Crossing the border was
their only hope so far as making good a final escape was
concerned. Sutton's worry dealt with whether they would
feel it necessary to alter their route.

The fact that he had a hostage in Olive Bain, and possibly Amy Starr, had given Rufe supreme confidence in the

belief that he would not be challenged during the journey to the border. If that assurance did not wane Tom figured he could expect to find the outlaws and the girls somewhere along the road. Should the opposite prove true, however, then it would become apparent he had lost the fleeing party and he would be faced with doubling back, searching out the trail left by four horses, and continuing from there; and that would mean waiting for daylight.

Tom stirred wearily on his saddle as the bay pressed steadily on through the night. Rufe had played it smart; he had figured on the darkness to lay a blanket of cover over his movements and make pursuit, should anyone try, doubly difficult.

The gelding veered suddenly in stride as a dark shape bolted abruptly from a clump of oak. Grabbing the saddlehorn to keep from losing his seat, Sutton swore wryly. It had been a coyote, or perhaps a wolf, down from the higher levels of the Muleheads. The bay had almost run over the animal.

In the next moment Tom Sutton came to attention. Holding the horse to a slow walk, he listened into the night. From off to the left, in the direction of the road, came the drumming of running horses. It was not possible to judge the number, but it was no lone rider, he was certain of that. Was it the Avery brothers hurrying to overtake him—or was it Rufe and his party?

19

Olive Bain allowed the reins of the horse she was riding to hang slack while she steadied herself by gripping the saddlehorn. The stirrups, adjusted to fit the legs of J. J. Levitt, were much too long, and the outlaws had not seen fit to shorten them. But she was no worse off than Amy; the girl was having a bad time of it as, clinging to Deke, she struggled to hold her place on the back of his saddle while they pounded on through the night.

Matters were somewhat better, however. At the start Rufe had insisted they stay off the road and ride a parallel course. The ground had been rough and broken, and keeping from falling from her horse had been a nightmare since she could find no solid purchase for her feet. But finally the outlaw had chosen to swing back onto the established trail, convinced no doubt they could make faster time.

Nevertheless, they would have to halt soon. The horses were tiring, evidently having been ridden hard before they arrived in Mimbres Crossing. Olive sighed. She would be glad when Rufe gave the signal to pull up. At least then she could do something about the stirrups. She'd ask Deke to shorten them for her. He didn't seem such a bad sort.

She must try to delay Rufe as much as possible once they had halted. Tom Sutton was following them; he'd said nothing to her while they were in the schoolhouse, but the look he'd given her had been meaningful and conveyed the thought. Tom would be coming, of that she was certain.

Olive turned again to Amy. The girl's arms were around Deke, her head was pressed against the back of his shoulders and she sought to ride with the motion of the horse. Amy was near exhaustion, that was evident.

"We've got to stop," Olive said firmly, shifting her attention to Rufe. He was to her left a short distance and she was forced to raise her voice in order to be heard above the hoofbeats.

The outlaw touched her with a cold, disdainful glance and made no reply, but beyond him the older man, Al, heard and nodded.

"She's right, Rufe. Ain't no sense running these horses into the ground. Best we pull up for a couple of hours."

Rufe turned and looked over his shoulder. The moon was out, and complemented by the glittering stars, was casting a sheen of silver over the land. The road along which they had just come was well lighted for some distance.

"You worrying about a posse?" Al asked, also twisting about to study their back trail.

"Just having me a look-see," Rufe answered, coming back around. "I'm pretty sure there ain't no posse going to bother us but that there sheriff—I ain't so certain about him."

"Him by hisself? What could he do?"

"Maybe nothing, but I ain't giving him no chance to try."

"Looks like some bluffs up ahead," Al said then. "We could pull off the road, find us a good place where nobody'd see—"

"Rufe," Deke broke in, "we stopping pretty soon? Amy's kind of shook up and ain't feeling so good."

The outlaw leader swore, brushing angrily at his face. "All right, but while we're resting the horses you fix it so's she can ride—hear? I ain't got time to mess around with her."

Deke mumbled something in reply, and then shortly Rufe, pulling slightly ahead, swung from the road and began to veer toward a shadowy wall of hills to their right.

Olive sighed thankfully. A couple of hours, or even one off Levitt's horse, would come as a big relief for her—and for Amy. A frown drew her brows together. Halting could bring about serious problems, she realized, and began to give thought as to what she could do if Rufe got ugly. Al probably would pose no threat, nor would Deke who was so wrapped up in Amy Starr, but she doubted she could look to either of them for help. Rufe was a killer, as he'd demonstrated by cold-bloodedly shooting down Levitt. Both men feared him.

The young teacher smiled grimly. She had no weapon of course, and against a brute like Rufe she would probably be unable to make use of one, if she did; it was best to remain quiet, keep out of the outlaw's way—and hope.

They drew up in a small hollow in the base of the first bluff and as they all dismounted, Rufe handed the reins of his horse to Deke.

"Look after the animals, kid," he said, and then laughed. "That is, if you can pry yourself loose from your woman."

Deke grinned broadly, and collecting the reins of their mounts, led them off into a stand of nearby brush. Olive, moving quietly in the pale darkness to where Amy was standing, noting as she did the exact location where the young outlaw was picketing their mounts, placed her arm around the girl.

"Are you all right?"

"A little shaken up," Amy admitted hesitantly. "It was hard to ride that way. I—I hope we can stay here for a while."

"So do I," Olive murmured, and cast a covert glance at Rufe and Al. They had drawn off to themselves on the opposite side of the small clearing fronting the bluff, and were engaged in conversation. She turned back to the girl.

"Amy, we've got to try and escape. You keep watching me—be ready. I'll try to get to the horses when no one's looking, and when the chance comes, I'll lead two off to the side, turn the others loose and then we—"

"No," Amy Starr said quietly. "I don't want to go back. I love Deke—I want to be with him."

"But he's an outlaw—"

Amy smiled. "That doesn't matter, Miss Bain. What he is makes no difference to me. I guess you could say I've found what I want in life, and while maybe it isn't all you said we should look for, I feel happy."

"But you're so young—how can you be sure you love him?"

"I just know, that's all, and Miss Bain, I think you were wrong about one thing—"

"What was that?"

"All those things about being particular and choosing just the right man who could give you a fine life and such—that isn't so. I don't believe you can make yourself love any man. I've found out that when you meet the one who's right for you, you'll fall in love with him right then and there no matter who or what he is."

Olive was silent for a long breath, her thoughts in tur-

136

moil. Then, "But I don't see," she began, and once again fell quiet as Deke emerged from the brush.

"You getting yourself rested up?" he asked, putting his arm around the girl.

Amy nodded, and together they moved off. From across the clearing Olive heard Al say: "Got some coffee in my saddlebags. It all right to build a fire, make a pot?"

"No fire," Rufe answered flatly.

He wheeled abruptly, walked to the edge of the open ground and stared off in the direction of the road. Apparently satisfied after a moment that no one was coming, he retraced his steps, halting in the center of the clearing.

"We're laying up here for maybe an hour or so. No more'n that. Horses'll be ready by then, everybody else best be ready too."

He was directing his words to her, Olive realized, as well as at Deke and Amy, and turning, she moved off at once, breaking the steady push of his eyes fixed upon her, and finding a flat rock at the edge of the brush, sat down.

"I've been thinking," Al's whining tones came to her again. "That money; I still figure it'd be smart to divvy it up. I got a idea we ought to be splitting and all of us heading out on our own."

"What's wrong with staying together till we get to Mexico?" Rufe asked indifferently.

"We got all day tomorrow ahead of us before we come to the border. We're bound to be seen by somebody if the word's out. Four horses'll be spotted mighty quick. Man riding alone ain't going to be noticed."

"Al's right," Deke said, coming up from the fringe of brush where he and Amy had been standing. His arm still encircled the girl as if he feared he might lose her. "I'd kind of like having my share now."

137

"You'll get it," Rufe said.

"We could take it a mite easier too," Deke continued. "It's real hard on Amy, us having to ride the way we're doing."

"It was you that brought her along—"

"I know that, but I figure we're far enough from that town now and can sort of let up a bit, 'specially if we do like Al wants and head out in different directions."

Rufe stirred irritably. "I'll do some thinking on it," he said.

Al muttered something and shrugged. Deke, with Amy now holding to his hand, sauntered toward the shallow cave in the base of the bluff where they sat down in the loose dust.

The night was quiet, and Olive, straining to hear the sounds that would indicate the coming of Tom Sutton, held herself motionless in the shadows falling across the rock upon which she sat. There was nothing to encourage her—only the far-off yelping of coyotes, the hooting of an owl somewhere up on top of the bluff and the nearby rustling of dry leaves beneath a creosote bush where some small animal foraged for food.

She would not hear Tom when he came, she realized after a time. He would approach carefully, quietly—but he would come. Her faith in that was unshaken. Tom would not let her remain a captive of the outlaws to do with as they wished; he would rescue her and he would do so before any harm could befall her—Amy, too, if she wished.

Amy . . . She had always been a bit on the romantic side, a dreamer and wholly dissatisfied with life on her father's ranch. It was only natural she would believe all of the things Deke had probably whispered to her. He could be only playing with her, letting her think he wanted to make her his wife. The chances were that Amy was a little better off insofar as their future in the hands of the outlaws was concerned than she, Olive thought.

Or could Amy Starr be right? Had she been wrong in her outlook on life? Could it be true that love was all that mattered, that happiness could not come from material things but only from—

"Something else—"

Al's voice, harsher than earlier, broke into Olive's thoughts. She turned to listen.

"When're we dumping them women? They're holding us back, and there ain't no use us taking any more chances than we have to."

"Ain't slowed us down yet," Rufe said.

"Maybe not, but it's coming. That teacher's having hell on J.J.'s horse and the little one riding double with the kid's all but give out. He'll be belly-aching to stop for her every mile or two." Al paused briefly, then went on. "Another good reason why it'd be smart to divvy up the cash. The kid could take off with the little one, do what he wanted."

"You sure got that stuck in your mind, ain't you?"

"I just don't want something going wrong after we got this far. Getting shed of the teacher and letting the kid go on with his gal would be a load off'n us, I figure."

"I was thinking we ought to hang onto the teacher, leastwise till we was across the line."

Al swore. "What for? Dammit, Rufe, you're asking for trouble. It's a far piece to Mexico yet and we ain't for certain the law won't be waiting somewheres between here and there."

Rufe hawked, then spat. "You're worse'n an old woman when it comes to worrying—"

"Could be, but it's kept me living," Al snapped. Abruptly, he added: "Hell, I'm quitting you, Rufe. I'll take my share of the money right now and head out. Then you can do what you damn please."

Shifting the saddlebags containing the ransom from a shoulder to his hand, Rufe shrugged resignedly. "All right," he said, indifferently. "Get the kid and we'll do the splitting up. Count it out over there on that big rock."

Olive, pulse quickening, watched the outlaw turn, and with his back to her, moved toward a large boulder at the edge of the bluff. She would never have a better opportunity to escape, she realized, as Al, too, turned his attention to Deke. She only wished there was something she could do for Amy, but persuading the girl to accompany her appeared hopeless. Crouched low, she started for the horses.

20

The hammer of hoofs faded gradually, becoming inaudible. Tom, with the bay at a slow walk through the cool, moonlight-shot darkness, continued to puzzle over possibilities; was it Pete Avery and his brother, Gabe? Could he have caught up with Rufe and his party? Or was it only pilgrims compelled, for some reason, to do their traveling at night?

He discarded the latter. People didn't ordinarily travel after dark. The roads at best were often indefinite and under the soft, deceptive glow from the heavens which altered shape and seemingly substance; it was easy to go astray and become lost.

And the Averys. . . . They would have ridden hard and fast to draw abreast. Too, there was the strong likelihood that Pete, never known to involve himself in anything where there was work concerned, could have given it up and turned back. But that was only a hope; Pete Avery was carrying a big grudge now and that could be pushing him to break the usual pattern of his life.

And it was logical to believe that, having cut across country, he had overtaken Rufe and the others by that time; and if his calculations were correct, and he continued on the same, mile-saving course, he should find himself well ahead of them within another half hour or so and in a position to establish his ambush.

It had to be the outlaws and their hostages he had heard, Sutton decided, and setting spurs to the bay, he broke the big horse into a fair lope and pressed on, pointing for the bluffs several miles in the distance.

When the end of the ragged line of embankments finally began to loom up darkly in the pale night, Sutton slowed the gelding, and changing direction, swung toward the formations from the front. Again relying on his own calculations, he believed he was there well ahead of Rufe and his party, but it would be wise to approach quietly, taking no chances.

Playing it safe and assuming the hoofbeats he'd heard were those of the outlaws' horses, was only wise. It was entirely possible he had reached the bluffs after the party had passed—or that they were somewhere in the near vicinity. That Rufe had lost no time putting distance between Mimbres Crossing and himself despite his expressed confidence that no posse would dare pursue, was clearly evident.

The first of the palisades, rising like a shadowed, rough-faced wall in the night, was slightly to his left. Sutton halted, considering the advisability of crossing the wide, brush-filled arroyo that lay in front of it, or approaching it by first riding a parallel course along the bank of the wash and swinging in from the side. By following the latter route he could move in unseen—a precaution that might or might not be necessary.

But he had a feeling about the area, a deep-seated uneasiness, and in accordance with his own practice of heeding intuition as well as obeying mentor Luke Jones's advice to never ignore a hunch, Tom continued along the edge of the wash, moving as silently as possible through the clumps of rabbit brush, plume and other growth. He had planned to do his waiting at the upper end of the bluff, at a point that overlooked the road, but now he was not sure—

The sound of a horse stamping wearily brought Tom Sutton up short. It had come from across the arroyo, and back toward the bluff. Senses taut, he slipped from the saddle. Winding the bay's reins about the limb of a squat cedar, he removed his spurs and hung them on the saddle-horn. Drawing his gun, he eased down into the wash and began to work his way across while the question, *Could it be the outlaws, certain they had not been followed, had halted for the night?* hung in his mind.

He had covered little more than half the distance when the deep tones of men's low voices came to him. Immediately he hunched behind a thick clump of creosote bush, straining to pick up the words being said. He was too far away and failed to establish the identities of the speakers. It could be Rufe and his partners, or it could be someone else.

Again the horse, now to his left in a dense stand of growth, stirred restlessly. Tom guessed he was coming in to the camp from a point below it and the picketed mounts —which was a bit of luck. Any noise created by him would be attributed to the horses. A tight smile on his lips, he moved on.

It was the outlaws. The last bit of doubt in Sutton's mind vanished and a flow of relief filled him as he peered through the veil of brush fringing the small clearing at the base of the cliff. Rufe's voice reached him; the outlaw was saying something about being worried—or perhaps he was accusing Al or the boy, Deke, of becoming a worrier. The reply he received was quiet and Tom failed to catch the words but he thought the voice was that of the older man, Al.

"All right," Rufe said then, "get the kid and we'll do the splitting up. Count it out over there on that big rock."

The outlaws had apparently decided to separate and were preparing to divide the ransom money. It would be the ideal time to move in on them while they were thus engrossed. Tom frowned, reconsidering the thought; where were Olive and Amy Starr? There'd been no mention of them and no indication of their presence.

"Hey, kid, get over here—"

It was Al's voice. Tom drew himself upright. Parting the heavy growth, he endeavored to see the area at the base of the bluff where the outlaws had halted. It was closed off to him by more brush, the only portion visible being the upper part of the formation at the base of which, he recalled, was a small hollowed-out cave.

The men would be there where it would be natural to make camp. Chances were the two girls were being held inside the cave. That was good—they would be out of harm's way. Dropping low to keep from being silhouetted against the night, Sutton circled the brush clump and edged forward. He would be coming up to the outlaws from the rear, and since there was a prevalence of rocks and scrubby growth, the advantage would all be his. With the odds three to one, he thought grimly, he'd need it.

He reached the horses; four of them tied to a mesquite near the foot of the bluff. Heads down, utterly worn out from the fast, hard ride from Mimbres Crossing, they were dead beat. Rufe had been forced to halt—a possibility Tom had given thought to earlier, and then ruled out as being unlikely. Now he wondered if the outlaws' intention was to wait for morning before riding on; if so, should he, too, delay until daylight? Visibility would be no problem then and the risk and dangers involved in confronting three desperate men would be considerably lessened.

Rufe's holding over for any great length of time didn't seem logical. The outlaw had proven that his confidence in making an unchallenged escape was not as strong as he'd implied. Most likely he'd give the horses only a couple of hours to recover and then they would ride on, either together or each taking a different course. He'd best make his move now; darkness worked both ways—in his favor as well as theirs.

Circling the spent horses, Sutton continued, now moving with extreme care. He reached the last line of brush and gained the point where he could see the cleared space fronting the bluff and the hollow gouged from its face.

He drew back suddenly. A figure had appeared among the rocks to his left, rising out of the shadows to stand, partly crouched, in the meager light. Sutton took a long breath. It was Olive Bain.

He watched the girl as she hesitated, eyes on the three men he would now see hunched over something—the saddlebags, he supposed—near the cave. Then, turning carefully, the girl began to make her way toward the nearby horses.

Tom frowned, settling back. Olive would pass only an arm's length below him. He must stop her—but do so without frightening her and causing her to cry out.

"Hey—where'd the teacher go?"

At Rufe's expected shout, Olive froze. Tom, hunched

145

below the top of the brush and scattering of rocks, could no longer see the outlaws, but the quick crunch of boot heels in the sandy soil warned him they were hurrying toward the girl—and him.

21

"Where you think you're going?" Rufe shouted angrily, grabbing Olive by the arm and jerking her around. "You trying to run out on me—that it?"

"I was," the girl answered boldly.

"Well, think again, Missy," the outlaw snarled, and half dragging her, started back for the clearing.

From close by Al said: "I told you it'd be smart to get shed of her. She won't be nothing but trouble."

"Maybe I like her kind of trouble," Rufe snapped. "I'll get rid of her when I'm damn good and ready. Ain't none of your butt-in anyways if you're still aiming to take off on your own."

"I'm still aiming," Al said laconically, watching Rufe jerk and shove the girl toward the hollow in the bluff.

Sutton, controlling the anger that pulsed through him, unable to do anything for fear of making it worse for Olive, waited tensely. He could make no move until the outlaw had released the girl and she was well away from him. But he'd hold back no longer after that; Rufe's savage treatment of Olive had infuriated him and the knuckles of the hand clutching his pistol were white from strain.

"Now, damn you—stay there where I can keep a eye on you!" the outlaw ordered, shoving the girl toward the cave.

Olive went down, sprawling into the loose dust and gravel, but she made no outcry, simply lying motionless under Rufe's hard stare. Then, when he turned back to the rock upon which the saddlebags lay, she picked herself up slowly. Amy Starr appeared at that moment. She came from inside the cave, knelt beside Olive, and taking her by the arm, helped her to her feet.

Al and Deke, following Rufe, gathered again at the rock. The oldest of the three laughed admiringly.

"That there teacher gal's got more spunk than I figured!"

Rufe paused to look back at the girl. "Sort of surprised me some too. Maybe I done a better job of picking than I thought."

Sutton, once more upright, waited impatiently while Amy and Olive Bain moved into the cave and were lost in the shadows. Both appeared to be worn and near exhaustion but no worse than that; another manhandling or two by Rufe, however, and it would be a different matter.

Delaying another long minute to make certain everything in the clearing had settled down, Tom Sutton moved forward through the brush, quietly skirting the larger rocks and placing each step carefully so as to avoid the dry leaves and other litter on the sun-baked soil while keeping himself out of sight as much as possible.

Luck was again favoring him and taking all three of the outlaws shouldn't be too difficult, he thought. They were clustered around the boulder upon which lay the saddlebags. Three stacks of money were near the leather pouches, and as Rufe moved to resume the distribution of the cash, he paused to consider Deke.

"I was noticing you sort of hung back when me and Al went after the teacher," he said. "Wasn't so's you'd have time to do a little finagling with them piles of cash, was it?"

The young outlaw stiffened. "Hell, no! I never touched nothing! You saying I—"

"I ain't saying nothing, just wondering," Rufe cut in. "Can damn quick find out, I reckon, just by doing a little counting again, and if I find my pile short—"

"Never mind," Tom Sutton said, moving into the clearing. "It won't make any difference now."

Rufe reacted instinctively. He lunged to the side, drawing his weapon as he spun—all in one amazingly fast motion.

Sutton, weapon already out and leveled, fired coolly. The bullet caught the outlaw in the chest before he could complete the turn, driving him back against the rock behind him.

The lawman triggered his weapon once more as he saw Rufe, driven by sheer will, raise his pistol again despite the bullet he had taken, and pivoted fast. There was no time to wonder if Rufe would have the strength to get off the shot, he had to face Al now bringing up his gun.

Both his pistol and that of the older outlaw exploded. Tom felt the whip of Al's slug as it ripped through the sleeve of his brush jacket. Cool, he thumbed back the hammer of his forty-five, preparing to get off another shot.

There was no need as far as Al was concerned. The outlaw staggered as Tom's heavy-caliber bullet drove into him, and already dead, he was falling face down into the dust; Sutton's sharp, drilling attention was centered on Deke. The younger man was standing motionless, hand poised above the pistol untouched in the holster on his hip. He seemed paralyzed, unable to move.

A shrill cry came from Amy Starr as she burst suddenly from the cave. Through the thin layers of drifting powder

smoke, Tom saw her run to Deke's side, and heedless of all
else, throw her arms about him.

"No!" she screamed. "No!"

Sutton, aware that Olive Bain had also come from the
shadowy hollow in the bluff and was watching him intently, eased forward slowly, pistol still ready. He drew up
a long stride in front of the outlaw.

"What's it to be, Deke?"

For answer Amy Starr wheeled, placed herself protect-
ingly before the man. "Don't kill him—please! He's not like
them—he's different!"

"An outlaw—same as they were—"

"No—no he's not!" the girl cried. "He just fell in with
them a while back. He hasn't done anything bad."

Tom Sutton's jaw hardened as a quick vision of Luke
Jones slowly bleeding to death as he lay sprawled on the
ground back in the picnic grove at Mimbres Crossing
passed through his mind.

"No, nothing but take a hand in killing a good lawman
and holding up a town for ransom," Sutton said caustically. "Make up your mind, Deke. Either push her out of
the way and go for that gun—or raise your hands."

"It wasn't him that shot Sheriff Jones," Amy continued
in a high, frantic voice. "It was Rufe. He killed that other
man—Levitt—too."

Tom nodded coldly at the three piles of money on the
rock. Olive was now at his side.

"He was taking his share of the ransom money just the
same."

"I know—but he would've given it back! I was going to
make him when—"

Deke abruptly lifted his arms and stepped from behind

the girl. "Reckon there ain't no use of me saying anything, Sheriff. It's all been said."

"Keep coming," Sutton ordered in a cold, flat voice. He was totally unmoved by either the girl's pleas or the young outlaw's repentance.

Rigid, gun unwavering, he allowed Deke to draw close, and then reaching out he lifted the man's weapon from its holster. Stepping back he thrust it under his waistband. Only then did he turn to Olive Bain.

"You all right?"

She nodded. "Tired—frightened, but I'm fine now. I—I was never so glad of anything in my life as I was to see you, Tom."

He felt her arms slip around his middle, heard the faint sob of relief that escaped her lips. Something within him stirred and he wondered if there was affection in her actions or was she merely showing her gratitude?

"It's all over now," he said gruffly. "Go to the horses, look and see if you can find some rope or cord in the saddlebags. I'll have to tie up Deke."

"He won't try to run away!" Amy protested. "I promise that. You'll promise, too, won't you, Deke?"

The outlaw stared at the girl, a puzzled look on his face. He shrugged. "Sure, I'll promise."

"You see?"

Sutton smiled disinterestedly, motioning for Olive to do as he had requested.

"I give you my word, Sheriff," Deke said, "if that'll mean anything to you. I'm aiming to start all over."

"No, it's not good enough for me," the lawman replied.

"There's still no need for it," Amy insisted, beginning to weep.

The outlaw lowered his arms slowly, questioningly, eyes

on Tom. When no objection came he placed his hands on the girl's shoulders, turning her about.

"It's all right, Amy. Sheriff's right in doing what he has to. If it was me in his boots I'd feel the same way."

"But you haven't done anything real bad—killed anybody, I mean—"

"Maybe not, but I was mixed up in it—and like he says I was taking my share of the money. It was for us, Amy. I want you to believe that. We needed it so's we could go off somewheres and get started."

"I know that—and it's not fair that you—"

Tom glanced around as Olive returned, halting beside him with a short piggin string in her hand. She offered the bit of small-diameter rope to Sutton.

"This was all I could find—"

"It'll do fine," he said, and taking it from her, directed Deke to put his hands behind his back. Stepping in close, he bound the outlaw's wrists together.

"What are you going to do with him?" Amy asked in a trembling voice.

Sutton, punching the empty cartridges from his weapon and reloading, shrugged. "Take him back to town. He'll have to stand trial."

Amy, tears flowing afresh, threw herself on the young outlaw.

"Don't worry, Deke!" she sobbed. "I'll get pa to help. He's got a lot of friends, and he'll get you pardoned or freed—somehow."

Deke made no reply, staring off woodenly into the fading night. Sutton reached out, took him by the arm, and thrusting the girl aside gently, pushed him toward a nearby rock.

"Sit there," he directed. "I've got to get that money

back into those saddlebags, and then load your friends onto their horses. Be first light by that time and we can head back for town."

Sutton started to wheel to ask Olive to keep watch over Amy, and see that she tried nothing foolish—but halted. Guns drawn, Pete and Gabe Avery were standing at the edge of the clearing.

22

"Don't you worry none about that money," Pete said thickly through his bruised and swollen lips. "Me and Gabe'll take care of it."

Sutton watched the Averys advance slowly. He shook his head. "Smartest thing you can do is put away those guns and back off."

"We're doing the smart thing," Gabe said, grinning. "Lot of cash there."

"And it ain't but a couple of jumps to the border," Pete added. "Luck's finally a-coming our way, little brother. Get them hands up higher, Deputy, unless you want me to blow your head off!"

Tom, arms raised, studied the pair closely. With pistols drawn and ready, rushing them was out of the question. He must bide his time, wait for an opportunity to act. At this stage of the game, with Rufe and his gang of outlaws accounted for, the ransom recovered, he was not about to permit the Avery brothers to take over.

"Get the cash, dump it back into them saddlebags," Pete directed. "I'll keep a eye on the deputy."

Gabe holstered his weapon and shambled hurriedly to the rock where Rufe had been dividing the money into equal shares. The glare of dawn was now becoming noticeable in the east and the shadows along the foot of the bluff were already disappearing. Overhead crows were straggling across the lightening sky, having deserted their roosts in the hills and heading now for feeding grounds up the valley.

"You plug them two?" Pete Avery asked, pointing at the sprawled figures of Rufe and Al.

Tom nodded. "That's how you'll end up—you, too, Gabe —unless you forget—"

"Ain't likely," Pete cut in. "We'll be lining out for Mexico, and we'll get there before anybody knows what happened." He paused, jerking his head at Deke. "How's it come he ain't dead too?"

"Got sense enough to know he couldn't beat the law."

Pete laughed. "Reckon that always depends on whose got the drop on who. . . . Gabe, you about ready?"

The younger Avery, buckling the straps on the now refilled leather pouches, bobbed.

"Sure am," he said, and wheeling, moved back to Pete's side. "We can head out any time. What'll we do with him?" he continued, attention on Sutton.

"Well, I don't figure on letting him trail after us! You rustle up some rope. We'll hog-tie him so's he can't get loose—that other jasper too."

Gabe passed the saddlebags to his brother, started to turn away, but then hesitated. Glancing at Olive and Amy he said, "Be needing rope for them, won't we?"

"No, I've been doing a little figuring there," Pete drawled. "We're taking them right along with us—just like them others was aiming to do."

Gabe's stubble-covered face lit up happily. He winked broadly at Amy Starr. "Now, that's a real good idea, Pete! Us having us some female company while we're—"

"No!"

Deke's shout was like the sharp crack of a bullwhip.

155

Lunging, he charged straight at the two men, yelling as he went. Pete and Gabe, startled, came about to face the young outlaw. In that small fragment of time Sutton's arm swept down. Metal glinted in his hand. The weapon he suddenly held blasted, shattering the early morning hush, its shocking report blending with that from Pete Avery's gun.

Amy Starr screamed as Deke rocked sideways and went down. Sobbing wildly, she rushed to him. A few steps away Pete had sunk to his knees, life gone. Sutton pivoted to Gabe Avery, fired again as the younger of the two brothers was leveling his pistol. Gabe staggered and fell heavily.

In the cold, gray light with gunsmoke once again hovering about him like pale mist, Tom Sutton stood motionless. A heaviness settled through him. The town should be well satisfied now. The money and girls were safe, four men were dead by his hand, another wounded—perhaps dying —two more back in Mimbres Crossing to be buried—those latter not of his making, perhaps, but linked, nevertheless, in some way to him and the job he had assumed.

If this is the lot of a lawman, he thought bleakly, *I'm not sure I want it.*

"You had to do it, Tom—"

Olive's soft voice registered on Sutton's consciousness. As if reading his mind, she was striving to allay the bitter doubts that assailed him.

"Deke's bad hurt! Help us—please!"

Amy Starr's frantic plea removed the last barrier to Sutton's return to reality. Glancing down at Olive, he put his arm around her, pressed her firmly to his side for a brief moment. Then, holstering his pistol he crossed to where the outlaw lay. Kneeling beside the girl he opened Deke's blood-stained shirt and examined the wound.

"Is—is it bad?" Amy asked in a breathless, strained voice.

"Bad enough—but he'll be all right if we get him to Doc Kenneman," the lawman replied. "Find something for bandages—your petticoat'll do. Make a pad and put it over the place where the bullet went in. Then tie a—"

"Here, let me do it," Olive broke in, dropping to her knees.

Amy shook her head. "No," she said quietly, reaching for her underskirt. "I'll take care of him—he's my man." And then, as Sutton rose and turned away to make the necessary preparations for the return to Mimbres Crossing, she added: "You look after yours."

Olive Bain frowned, drew herself erect and glanced toward Tom Sutton as he moved off. Abruptly she smiled.

"That's what I intend doing—from now on," she replied, and hurried to catch up with him.